QUIET HEROES

STORIES FROM THE FRONTLINES OF THE VIETNAM WAR

LARRY BURKE

Quiet Heros: Stories from the Frontlines of the Vietnam War

ISBN- 978-1-964081-89-2 paperback
ISBN: 978-1-964081-41-0   eBook
Library of Congress case no. 1-14896435931

Published by: HigherLife Development Services, Inc.
PO Box 623307
Oviedo, FL 32762
(407) 563-4806
www.ahigherlife.com

Printed in the United States of America
10 9 8 7 6 5 4 3 2 1

Thank you to Carl Delberta for your continuing support and friendship, Jeff Wagner for your encouragement and Gary and Michelle for helping bring this book to print.

CHAPTER 1

HOCKEY TO THE FRONT LINES

"We're under attack."

The pilot's voice broke through the intercom as the plane descended into Vietnam. For a moment, I thought I misheard him.

Under attack? We weren't even on the ground yet. Around me, the other guys looked just as confused—until the first explosion hit. The floor beneath us shook, and suddenly, it wasn't confusion I saw in their faces—it was fear. Real, bone-deep fear.

Welcome to the war, Larry, I thought to myself.

This wasn't a dream. This wasn't supposed to be my life. I was supposed to be chasing pucks, not dodging explosives.

As the explosions rattled the plane, I couldn't help but think about how far I'd come—from the cold, clean lines of an ice rink to the heat and chaos of a war zone. It didn't make sense. None of it did. My life was supposed to be simple. Hockey was supposed to define me, not this. Not Vietnam.

Ever since I could lace up a pair of skates, that's where my heart was. Fast on the ice and sharp with a hockey stick, I had one goal—make it big in hockey. Forget school. Forget anything else. It was hockey or nothing.

By the time I hit eighteen, I was playing semi-pro. That was the dream. I wasn't the biggest guy on the ice—hell, I wasn't even close, coming in at just five feet six inches—but I made up for it with speed and guts.

The bigger guys thought they could push me around. I let them believe that until they were flat on their backs, looking up at the scoreboard.

That's how I liked it. Keep 'em guessing, keep 'em underestimating me. That's what got me on the team.

For a while, everything seemed like it was falling into place. I wasn't a regular starter, but I got to play. I believed my future was on the ice. But life has a funny way of knocking you down when you least expect it.

One day, you're chasing pucks on the ice, and the next, you're staring down a letter from Uncle Sam telling you your future doesn't involve a rink. It doesn't involve ice. It involves a jungle.

***

I was at the kitchen table when the draft notice came. My dad handed me the letter, his hand trembling a little. He didn't say anything—he didn't have to. I could see the worry in his eyes. He already knew what that letter meant, even before I opened it.

I tore it open, my hands now shaking a little, too, and there it was.

"August 16, 1969
To: Larry Burke
Greetings:
You are hereby ordered to report for induction into the Armed
Forces of the United States…"

I read it, but I barely processed it. As I looked up at my dad, a World War II veteran, a sinking feeling took over.

There he was, standing at the kitchen table, silent. This wasn't the pep talk I'd expected. Just a blank stare—this was something I'd have to figure out on my own.

"So… that's it?" I asked, trying to keep my voice steady. The words barely made it out of my mouth.

He nodded slowly, not looking at me directly. "Yup, same as it was for me almost 30 years ago. You get your orders, and you go."

No sympathy. No fatherly advice. Just a reminder that the world doesn't stop for dreams. In his eyes, this was a duty. My duty.

He never talked much about it, but I'd seen the scars it left, the nightmares that still woke him up in the middle of the night. And now it was my turn.

I nodded, more to myself than to him. "Yeah, I guess you're right."

But inside, I wasn't so sure. I wasn't ready for this. Hockey was my future—at least, that's what I'd thought. I wanted to argue, to say, "But I have plans." I wasn't ready to swap out my skates for combat boots.

But staring into my dad's eyes, I couldn't find any words. I saw the same look I'd seen when he'd woken up from one of his nightmares.

A look that said, "You go, you survive, you come home. That's it."

I took a deep breath, feeling the weight of his words settle. Whatever he'd left behind to go fight, I'd now have to do the same. I had no idea what was waiting on the other side.

***

I didn't walk into this decision with a smile on my face. The draft notice that August hit me like a slap. I wasn't out there volunteering to head overseas—I wanted to stay on the ice, maybe even delay things a little longer. But that was clearly wishful thinking.

We had to report to an induction center in Newark, New Jersey. It was one of those old government buildings that had seen its share of kids like me. We shuffled in with nervous hands and forced bravery. Everything felt cold and official, like a place where dreams get put to rest.

I approached the Navy recruiter, thinking, *Stay out of the Army, and definitely stay out of the Marines.*

I had heard of the Army guys crawling through enemy tunnels in the jungle and joining the Marines wasn't going to be any better. I couldn't shake this one TV segment I saw, showing guys squeezing through these nightmare-tight passageways, rifles held high, looking like they were one wrong turn away from disaster. My heart raced when I remembered it.

I knew with my size; they'd stick me right in those damn tunnels. No, thank you. I wanted something that might keep me alive.

If I had to go, I figured the Navy was my best bet. Ships, engines— that was my way to stay out of the jungle. I didn't want to end up crawling through tunnels in the Army or dodging snipers in the Marines.

When the Navy recruiter at the induction center said, "What'll it be, son?" I told him my answer.

"You sure about this, kid?" he asked, his voice gruff but not unkind. "It's a four-year hitch. You can still get drafted and serve less time in the Army."

I nodded. "I'm sure."

He handed me a clipboard with some paperwork. "All right then. Welcome to the Navy."

***

Boot camp at Great Lakes was its own special hell. The air was cold enough to burn, and the rain felt like needles against my skin. It wasn't the kind of cold you shake off with a jog; it was deep, unrelenting.

My boots would sink into the mud, the weight making each step a struggle. But every time I wanted to quit, every time I thought, *What the hell am I doing here?* I could hear my dad's words in my head: "You get your orders, and you go."

We marched until our feet were numb, crawled through wet dirt until it caked on our skin, our breaths coming out in puffs in the cold morning air. I was exhausted, but I kept going.

Somewhere in that mud, I realized with certainty—the rink, the cold air on the ice, the roar of the crowd—was gone. All I had now was this new reality, and I had to own it.

In some ways, boot camp reminded me of hockey. The same drills and drive to push through the pain and exhaustion.

The only difference was, this time, there was no puck at the end of the line—just more work.

We marched for miles, our boots sinking into the wet, frozen ground. The air was bitter, stinging my face as we ran through endless drills. I could hear the groans of the guys next to me, the shuffle of boots, and the bark of orders from the drill instructor.

I just kept my head down and pushed through it. After all, I'd spent my whole life skating through pain. This wasn't any different. Or so I thought.

I wasn't prepared for the emotional toll. There was a moment right before I graduated boot camp when it hit me. I was standing in formation, the cold wind hitting my face, listening to the drill instructor bark orders, when I caught a glimpse of myself in a window.

I looked... different. My hair was buzzed short, my uniform crisp and clean. I barely recognized myself.

Who the hell are you? I thought, staring at my reflection. The fresh lines in my face, the hardness I didn't recognize. I wasn't the kid with dreams of hockey glory. I was someone else now—a sailor. It hit me like a gut punch.

> *I wasn't the kid with dreams of hockey glory. I was someone else now*

Shit, I thought. *This is really happening.*

***

After boot camp, I got sent to Engineman A School, still at Great Lakes. Engines were my way out of combat, so I threw myself into the work. I learned to fix anything they put in front of me—generators, motors, anything that kept the Navy moving. I liked it.

There was something satisfying about taking something broken and making it run again.

One day, another guy and I rebuilt the motor for a Patrol Boat River, a PBR. We got it running, and I felt pretty damn proud of myself. But little did I know that was sealing my fate.

***

Not long after that, I got the orders. Vietnam.

Before we shipped out, we were sent to survival training at Coronado Island in San Diego. That was a joke. They ran us through some basic drills, and they were supposed to tell us what to expect. But I could tell something was off—it didn't feel real. It was all too clean and controlled.

Then, we went to Camp Pendleton for weapons training. That was something else. They handed us an M16, let us throw one grenade, and then sent us on our way. That was it.

"What the hell is this supposed to prepare me for?" I asked the guy next to me as we walked back from the range.

He just shrugged. "Beats me. Guess we'll find out soon enough."

Before we shipped out, the last thing we did was meet with a team of Navy SEALs. These guys didn't sugarcoat anything.

They listed every brutal way we could die and finished with, "If you make it past two weeks out there, you *might* make it longer." Surviving two weeks felt like an impossible milestone. This wasn't a hockey game where, whether you win or lose, you go home. If you lost this game, you didn't go home. And the odds were stacked against us.

***

We flew out of San Diego for Vietnam in late October. The flight was endless, with stops in Anchorage and the Philippines. At each stop, the flight crew changed, and each time, they got older. The fresh-faced stewardesses were replaced by women with hard lines on their faces, the kind that only come from seeing too much.

"Why the change?" I asked one of them as she handed me a coffee.

She smiled, a tight, knowing smile. "Hazard pay."

"Hazard pay?"

"Yeah, kid. You're flying into a war zone. They pay us extra for that."

My stomach flipped. Hazard pay. For flying into a war zone. I glanced out the window, watching the ground below shrink, feeling the gravity of what was happening. This wasn't a layover before a hockey game or a family visit. This was it. Every mile we flew and hour we passed took me deeper into this new and terrifying reality. I was heading into something I couldn't control.

***

As we approached Tan Son Nhut Air Base, all hell broke loose. We were still in the air when the pilot came over the intercom.

"We're not landing at the terminal," he said, calm but tense. "The base is under attack."

Under attack? My heart started pounding. Mortars, rockets, small arms fire—it was all happening as we came in to land.

Instead, they landed us out in the open, nowhere near any cover. As soon as the plane touched down, they rolled a truck with stairs out, and we were told to run.

When the doors of the plane opened up, the heat hit first. It was a wall of humid air that made it hard to breathe. But then came the sounds. You could see the tracer rounds in the sky, painting a trail of fire and smoke lighting up the sky.

These explosions seemed too close, too real. The whole place was alive with noise and fire in the sky, a level of intensity I wasn't ready for.

No weapons—just running out of the plane in our civilian clothes and a whole lot of fear.

I hit the ground running, my shoes kicking up dirt as I sprinted for a ditch.

We were barely off the plane when the flight crew pulled up the stairs and took off. They were making a U-turn right back to the Philippines. They needed to get out of there as soon as possible. This was a war zone.

"Get down!" someone shouted as we hit the ground, scrambling into the open air.

I did as I was told, my face pressed into the dirt, my heart racing in my chest. All around me, explosions echoed in the distance, and I could hear the crack of gunfire.

I didn't have a weapon—no one did. I didn't have a plan—no one expected this. I just had the urge to survive pounding in my chest. All I could do was press my body into the ground and hope I'd made it this far for a reason.

I thought to myself, *Two weeks. Just make it through two weeks.*

This wasn't hockey. This wasn't a game. No one here was going to save me. This wasn't boot camp, and there weren't any drill sergeants shouting orders.

This was life or death—I wasn't ready for it. If I wanted to get home, I'd have to figure out how to survive this brutal place.

***

Eventually, the attack subsided, and they rounded us up. Army guys went one way, Marines went another, and we Navy guys got herded into a barracks in Saigon.

That's where they handed me my first uniform—a plain green one, no camouflage.

Why am I wearing a green uniform? I thought. *I'm not staying in Saigon, more than likely.*

Those guys in Saigon didn't really have to worry about camouflage because they were in Saigon—the populous capital city of South Vietnam.

After that, they handed me an M16.

With no ammo.

I looked at the gun in my hand, then at the guy who'd just handed it to me.

"What the hell am I supposed to do with this?" I asked, raising an eyebrow.

He shrugged. "You stand watch on the roof."

"With no ammo? What am I supposed to do, throw my gun at them?"

"If anyone starts shooting, you come down and get some."

I stared at him, not sure if he was messing with me. "Yeah. Right. Like I'll have time for that."

He just laughed and patted me on the back. "Welcome to Vietnam."

***

Looking back now, I can see how fast everything changed. One day, I was chasing a dream on the ice, and the next, I was running for cover in a war zone. Life doesn't give you time to adjust; it throws you into the deep end, and you either learn to swim or you drown.

In those first weeks in Vietnam, I wasn't sure which way I'd go. I hadn't asked for this. I didn't want any of it—the draft notice, the boots, the empty rifle. But lying in that ditch with the sounds of war pounding in my ears, I understood one thing: If I wanted to make it home, I had to adapt. I had to survive. Just like my dad had said.

That night, lying on my cot, my mind raced with the images of tracer rounds and the distant pop of mortars. Then the memory of the ice rink, the feel of gliding on my skates. It felt like it belonged to someone else. And maybe, in a way, it did. Because here, in Vietnam, none of that mattered. Here, I was nobody's star player, nobody's hero.

I was just another sailor, learning fast that life doesn't care about your plans. It'll throw you curveballs, and you must learn to hit them or get left behind.

I had no idea where the next chapter of my life would take me—or how drastically it would rewrite who I thought I was. But the first glimpse came soon enough as the truck rattled toward my new base. And there, the reality of war hit me harder than ever.

***

A few days after arriving in Vietnam, I was shipped off to my first base—Nhe Be, about 25 miles outside Saigon. When I stepped off the truck and saw the base, it hit me. This was Vietnam. This was real.

Nhe Be was a different world. It was hot, the air thick with humidity. The base was nothing special—just a few buildings and the constant sound of engines grinding away in the background.

But there was something else too—a tension. You could feel it in the air, as if the whole place was holding its breath, just waiting for something to happen.

And it did.

CHAPTER 2

ROCKETS, ENGINES, AND FRUSTRATION

"So this is where they put the Navy," I muttered under my breath. It didn't seem real, like something out of a bad movie.

I stepped off the truck and took it all in. The first thing I noticed about Nhe Be was the smell. Diesel, sweat, and something else—something metallic and sharp that I couldn't quite place.

The humid air pressed down on me like a weight—it was suffocating. The base didn't have the same energy as Saigon, where the streets bustled with life even in the middle of a war. No, Nhe Be was different.

But it wasn't just the smell that got me; it was the chaos. The base sat on the edge of a major river, a hub of activity with dozens of Patrol Boat Rivers—PBRs—lined up along the docks. It wasn't what I expected, but it was impressive.

The road leading to the base, though? That was something else entirely. Bars and whorehouses lined both sides of the street, almost all the way to the gate. I stared, wide-eyed, as the few other sailors and I rolled past them.

When we finally stopped at the gate, we hopped down from the truck and approached the guard. Before I could even say a word, he barked at me like I was a threat.

"Who are you?" he snapped, his hand resting a little too tightly on his weapon.

I glanced around, my frustration bubbling up. "Look, I'm not the enemy," I said, motioning across the road. "If you're worried about someone blowing you up, look over there. The guy with a satchel of explosives could walk out of that bar and do it any second."

The guard stared at me for a long moment, his jaw tightening before he finally waved me through. "Don't cause trouble," he muttered.

I shrugged and walked past him, the scene sticking in my head. This place didn't just feel dangerous—it *was* dangerous. The weight of it settled into my chest like lead. Every step felt like it might be my last. I tried to shake it off, but the fear clung to me, as sticky as the humidity. But here I was, assigned to a PBR unit and dropped into the middle of it. It was almost laughable, really. This was my new life.

***

My boots sank into the mud as I walked. The sky hung low, covered in thick grey clouds that threatened rain but never quite delivered. The buildings were scattered and surrounded by barbed wire and guard towers. I wiped the sweat from my forehead and glanced around at the base.

"This is it, huh?" I muttered to myself, trying to shake the unease in my gut.

There wasn't much here. Just a few barracks, the mess hall, and the motor repair shop where I'd be working. It was a far cry from the rinks I'd grown up in—cold, clean lines replaced with the sticky heat and constant buzz of engines grinding in the background.

I could feel the other sailors' eyes on me, sizing me up and trying to figure out who the new guys were. Some nodded in greeting, and others just stared before returning to their tasks. There was tension in the air, an undercurrent of something unspoken, like everyone was waiting for the other shoe to drop.

We weren't there five minutes before a guy with a cigarette dangling from his mouth walked by. His uniform was sweat-stained and unbuttoned, his boots caked in mud. He didn't even bother to look at me as he passed.

"Welcome to the jungle," he said, his voice flat and tired. I didn't know it then, but those words would haunt me later.

The words hung in the air, more a warning than a greeting. The jungle wasn't just around us—it resembled the spirit of how the base functioned in the unpredictability of every moment.

***

They didn't give me a moment to settle in. The moment I stepped onto the base, the absurdity of military logic hit me square in the face.

Take my first watch duty, for instance. They handed me an M16— no ammunition. I stood there for a second, staring at the guy issuing weapons. "Uh, where's the ammo?"

He didn't even blink. "If you need it, come back and get some."

"Come back and get some?" I repeated. "What am I supposed to do in the meantime, throw the rifle at them?" *How is this the norm?* I wondered.

The guy shrugged and moved on as if I'd asked him where the bathroom was. So, there I was, patrolling the fence line with a gun about as useful as a stick. If someone had tried to climb over that fence, I wouldn't have been able to do a damn thing about it. I didn't question my orders, though. What was the point? This was just another example of military stupidity.

A chief—the guy running the PBR I'd been assigned to—found me. He was all business, barely giving me time to catch my breath.

He gave me a look; the kind that told me I was about to learn the hard way.

"We're heading out tomorrow night," he said, his voice low and firm.

I nodded, trying to process the sudden shift. "Yes, sir."

He gave me a look; the kind that told me I was about to learn the hard way. "You're the engineman. Your job is simple—keep the diesel motors running. At least one of them better be good enough to get us the hell out of the river if things go south."

As he spoke, I felt a strange mix of relief and pressure. I understood engines, at least. But knowing my hands could mean the difference between life and death for the whole crew was new.

Engines were something I understood, something that made this whole chaotic environment feel a little less overwhelming. I could take them apart, piece by piece, find the problem, and put them back together again. I clung to that. Because here, you had to focus on what you could control—and engines, at least, had some level of predictability. Now I had to make sure the engines *kept working* to save the lives of my countrymen. No pressure.

*****

The next night, I made my way to the boat. The base, for all its so-called precautions, was lit up like a damn Christmas tree—streetlights everywhere, like we weren't in the middle of a war zone. The brightness made it hard to adjust my eyes to the dark. When I finally got to the boat, I was still blinking away the glare, but I told myself it'd get better once we were out on the river.

The PBR was impressive—a 45-foot Chris Craft made specifically for Vietnam. Its V-shaped hull tapered off into a flat bottom, allowing it to glide through as little as 12 inches of water. It ran on two massive V6 diesel engines with enough torque to pull a house off its foundation.

The motors were loud, roaring even with covers that were supposed to muffle the sound. The vibrations from the engines weren't just physical—they got inside your head, a constant reminder of what kept us moving. Every hum and thrum felt like a pulse of life against the unknown. Fiberglass made up most of the boat's body—great for speed, terrible for protection. The only armored section was around the driver, the coxswain, and even that wasn't much.

We always ran our boats in pairs but never close together. The idea was to spread out so one hit wouldn't take out both boats. I climbed aboard and headed to the front, where the twin .50-caliber gunner was stationed.

"This ain't so bad," I said, leaning against the railing.

"Enjoy it while it lasts. Quiet doesn't stick around here for long." He smirked.

"Guess I'll take what I can get."

He barely got the words out when a B-40 rocket screamed out of the jungle, passing so close across our bow I could feel the heat from the blast. The gunner dove into position, gripping the twin fifties and unleashing hell on the jungle. Trees splintered, dirt exploded, and any-thing—or anyone—near the shoreline was shredded.

I scrambled to the back of the boat, my heart pounding as I checked the engines. My job wasn't to shoot unless absolutely necessary. My M16 was fully loaded this time, but I kept my focus on the motors. They had to stay running, or we were dead in the water.

Another rocket tore out of the jungle, this one aimed directly at us. I could see the fiery tail streaking toward the boat, and I clenched the railing so hard my knuckles turned white.

Go! I screamed inside my head, willing the driver to hit the throttle. He didn't. He just kept us coasting, calm as ever.

The rocket struck the armored section near the center of the boat. It bounced off, veered into the jungle, and exploded in the trees.

If the driver had sped up, it would've hit us midship and killed us all. I was yelling in my head for him to move, but he'd done the right thing.

Finally, he slammed the throttles forward. The boat dipped briefly, then surged ahead, the engines roaring as we tore down the river at 60 miles an hour. The jacuzzi pumps at the back sprayed water wide and steady, keeping us balanced as we sped along.

My hands gripped the railing. The jungle blurred past us as the engines roared—vibrations rattling through my boots. Every muscle in my body was tense, bracing for another hit. The air was thick with the smell of diesel and gunpowder, and I couldn't tell if the ringing in my ears was from the motors or the explosions.

The roar of the engines drowned out my thoughts, but the pounding of my heart was louder. The shift from fear to action was instant, but the fear left a lingering shadow.

How the hell am I still alive? I thought, glancing at the gunner, who was methodically scanning the tree line for movement. His face was calm and focused as if this were just another day at work. I envied him for that. My mind was a whirlwind of fear and adrenaline, my pulse racing as I waited for the next rocket.

Then, just as suddenly, we pivoted. The driver threw one motor into reverse, spinning the boat on a dime. I slid from one side to the other, slamming into the railing but somehow staying on board. We were now heading back the way we came.

As we headed back to base, the adrenaline began to wear off. My legs felt like jelly, my arms like lead. The motors hummed steadily behind me, a reminder that at least something was still working as it should.

I glanced at the other boat in the distance, watching as it turned to follow us. The crew was on the radio, likely warning the others about the rockets. My ears were ringing from the motors, but the sight of their calm, deliberate movements steadied me.

In the turmoil, an image hit me: my dad, sitting on the porch, telling me to serve and come home. His voice was calm and steady, the opposite of what I felt now. I wondered if he'd felt this same fear and adrenaline when he was out there. Maybe that's why he never talked about it. Some things are too big to put into words.

When we returned to base around one o'clock in the morning, my hands were still shaking. Two rockets in my first two weeks. I climbed off the boat, trying to catch my breath. The chief walked up, grinning like he'd just won a bet.

"We'll be off for a couple of days," he said casually. "I'll let you know when we're ready to go back out."

I nodded, not trusting myself to speak. Back at the barracks, I sank onto my cot and stared at the ceiling, the adrenaline finally wearing off. Two weeks in the country, and I was still alive. Barely.

***

The motor shop was a different beast altogether. It wasn't like being out on the PBRs, skimming down rivers with twin diesel engines roaring behind you. Here, everything was methodical and mechanical.

The motor shop had its own rhythm. Engines sputtered, tools clanged against metal, and the air smelled of grease and burnt oil. The Navy guys worked fast, their hands moving with precision as they stripped down motors and pieced them back together.

Boats came in beat to hell. Holes blasted through their fiberglass bodies, their engines sputtering or seized. The shop worked like a factory—cranes lifting damaged PBRs out of the water, swinging them around like toys, while teams of mechanics jumped in to fix what they could.

I remember watching one boat get hauled in on a crane, dangling over the water. I noticed a clean hole punched straight through the fiberglass as it swung toward the shop.

"B-40 rocket," someone muttered nearby. The projectile had hit the boat dead-on but didn't detonate—some mistake in the settings. Lucky for the crew onboard, but still a grim reminder of how fragile those boats really were. Every boat that came in told its own story—some with bullet holes peppering the hull, others barely holding together after rocket blasts.

I tried to keep my focus on the work. There was something oddly satisfying about pulling apart an engine, cleaning out the gunk, and making it run again. It was mechanical, predictable, and nothing like the uncertainty of the river.

But even here, the war found a way to creep in. The tension was palpable, buzzing through every conversation and glance across the shop.

Every time a boat came in, I couldn't help but imagine the faces of the crews who had been onboard. Some boats bore scars from close calls; others carried stories that would never be told. The shop became a sanctuary and a battlefield all at once.

***

A couple of days later, I was reassigned. The Navy had started transitioning most of the PBRs to Vietnamese crews, keeping only about ten boats for the U.S. Navy guys.

My boat didn't make the cut. After being here just over two weeks, I was reassigned to the motor shop to rebuild engines and teach Vietnamese workers how to do the same.

At first, it wasn't so bad. They paired me with a young Vietnamese kid—quiet, quick to learn, and good with his hands. We worked side by side for a few days, stripping engines down to their bolts, cleaning out gunked-up parts, and piecing them back together.

But one morning, he didn't show up.

He might've been sick or gotten reassigned. But as the hours passed and he didn't show, I started asking around. No one seemed to know where he was. Eventually, I found him in the injector shop, sitting on a workbench with a group of other Vietnamese workers, all laughing and chatting like they didn't have a care in the world.

I walked over, my frustration mounting. "You coming to work or what?" I asked.

He looked at me like I'd grown three heads. I knew he understood English—we'd been working together for days, and he'd picked it up well enough to communicate. But now, he just smirked and turned back to his buddies, ignoring me completely.

I tried again. "You gonna help me out, or am I doing this alone?"

No response. Just more laughter, more Vietnamese chatter.

Something snapped in me. Each laugh felt like a slap in the face. The sound carried an indifference I couldn't understand, like this war didn't touch them the way it touched us. My jaw tightened as frustration bubbled over.

Maybe it was the stress of the past two weeks—walking fence lines with no ammo, dodging rockets on the river, watching boats come back with holes blown through them. Or maybe it was the way he acted like none of this mattered, like it was all a game.

I thought of the guys on the PBRs, the ones putting their lives on the line every day while these kids sat here joking around. It wasn't just frustrating—it felt like a betrayal.

This isn't a game. This is a war zone. People are dying.

Without thinking, I walked up to him, grabbed him by the front of his shirt, lifted him clean off the workbench, and slammed him back down. Hard. I didn't say a word. I just turned and walked away, hoping maybe the jolt would wake him up to the reality of where we were and what was at stake.

As I headed back to the motor shop, an American officer came out of the office, his expression unreadable. "What's going on?" he asked.

"Nothing as far as I'm concerned," I said flatly, not breaking stride.

A few hours later, the same officer came to find me. Apparently, the Vietnamese workers had reported me for the incident. I was furious—not because they'd turned me in, but because they didn't seem to care about the bigger picture. We were supposed to teach them how to keep these boats running, not do all the work for them.

It wasn't just a boat on the line—it was people's lives. Every engine they neglected was one we might depend on in a fight, one that could mean the difference between coming back to base or not.

When they called me in to see the captain, I thought I had finally done enough to be sent home. I walked into his office and asked, "So, are you sending me home?"

"Home? Do you think this is a ticket out, Burke?"

I didn't answer, but I met his eyes, trying to hold onto whatever shred of dignity I had left.

He shook his head. "No. We're writing you up and sending you to another base."

And that was that. A few days later, I was reassigned to Roc Soi, a small base near the Cambodian border. From the shoreline, you could see Turtle Island—a little hump of land off the coast that looked exactly like its namesake. The proximity to Cambodia was no coincidence; even though they never publicized it, the Navy ran operations along the Ho Chi Minh Trail in that area.

As I packed my gear and prepared to leave, I couldn't shake the frustration. I didn't mind doing my part, but I hated feeling like the weight of everything was being dumped on me. People were dying out here, and too many of us treated it like a game.

Two weeks. That's all it had taken for the war to strip away any illusions I'd had. I came here thinking I knew how the world worked, but nothing about this place made sense. Orders didn't make sense. The unpredictability was constant. And sometimes, the people didn't make sense either.

But in the middle of all that, I'd learned something about myself. It wasn't about how fast I could run a mile or how many engines I could fix in a day. It wasn't even about how I handled the rockets or the Vietnamese workers. It was about knowing that no matter what this place threw at me, I could take it—and if I couldn't, I'd figure it out along the way.

Two weeks in, I learned survival wasn't just about staying alive. It was about finding a way to keep going when the world didn't make sense, when every part of you screamed to stop. It wasn't bravery. It wasn't heroism. It was just survival.

Somewhere out there, past the calm waters and distant tree lines, the next challenge waited for me.

I wasn't ready for it. Hell, I wasn't even sure what "ready" meant anymore. But I was still here, still breathing, still moving forward. And in a war like this, sometimes that's all you can ask for.

THE SWEET SMELL OF SURVIVAL

"Load your weapon. Lay in your bed. Stay quiet."

The SEAL's voice was low but firm, the kind of tone that created no space for disagreement. He didn't look at me as he spoke; his eyes scanned the dim room, his ears tuned to something I couldn't yet hear. My heart pounded, but I forced myself to nod, fumbling for my rifle.

"Something's wrong," I whispered, more to myself than to him.

"No kidding," he muttered, sliding a magazine into his weapon with practiced ease. "You hear that?"

I strained to listen, but all I caught was the faint creak of metal and a distant rustle. The alley outside, buzzing with life just an hour ago, was now silent. Too silent.

"I don't hear anything," I said.

"Exactly." He didn't elaborate; he didn't need to. The absence of noise—the kids playing, pots clanging, people laughing—meant only one thing: We were in trouble.

The SEAL motioned for me to stay where I was as he crept toward the doorway, his steps impossibly quiet despite the wooden floorboards. I followed his lead, settling into the far corner of the room, my rifle resting against my knee. My palms were slick with sweat, and I wiped them on my pants, trying to steady my breathing.

Then it started: a soft shuffle above us, like feet moving across the tin roof. The SEAL didn't hesitate. He raised his weapon and fired a single shot, the crack deafening in the enclosed space. A sharp metallic clang was followed by a thud as something, or someone, hit the ground outside.

"Got 'em," he said, his voice devoid of triumph. "But there's more."

"How many?" I asked, barely able to keep the tremor out of my voice.

"Doesn't matter. We're getting out of here."

He crossed the room in three quick strides, his presence commanding even in the dim light.

"We'll go back-to-back," he said, checking his weapon one last time.

"Stay close. Follow my steps. And if anything moves—anything— don't hesitate. You shoot. Got it?"

I nodded, though the thought of pulling the trigger on a dog, let alone a person, made my stomach churn.

We moved to the doorway, his back pressed against mine. Our rifles were raised and ready. The narrow, shadowed alley stretched out before us. Lined by old homes, it was empty, eerily so, the kind of emptiness that screamed trap.

The SEAL didn't say another word. He didn't need to. We moved in sync, step by step, the silence faintly broken only by the sound of our boots scraping against the dirt. My senses were on overdrive, every shadow a potential threat, every creak of wood a warning of disaster.

Halfway down the alley, something darted out from behind a pile of crates. I barely registered what it was—a blur of movement, too small to be a person. My rifle jerked up, my finger hovering over the trigger.

"Hold," the SEAL said, his voice cutting through my panic.

It was a thin cat whose eyes glowed in the dim light. It hissed and darted back into the shadows, disappearing as quickly as it had come.

"Let's go," he said, his tone urgent.

We reached the main road without incident, stepping into a scene that couldn't have been more different from the alley we'd just left. Cars cruised by, their headlights casting long shadows. Vendors called out to pedestrians, their voices loud and cheerful. It was as if the world had moved on, blissfully unaware of the danger lurking just a few steps away.

***

Roc Soi was unlike anything I had imagined when I first stepped foot in Vietnam. Instead of solid ground, the barracks floated on the river—two massive barges tethered to the shoreline. The air smelled of diesel, grease, and river muck, a cocktail of scents that clung to your skin and clothes no matter how many times you washed them.

Life on the base had its peculiar rhythm. By night, we lobbed percussion grenades into the water to fend off enemy swimmers who might plant explosives on the boats. The concussive blasts were deafening, capable of rupturing eardrums or worse if you were too close.

It was deadly and serious work, but like all things in war, it didn't take long for us to turn it into a game.

We'd lob the grenades high into the air, betting on who could make theirs explode mid-flight. "Your aim's worse than a blindfolded monkey," one guy would joke right before his own grenade hit the water with a disappointing splash.

Turtle Island loomed off the coast, its silhouette resembling its namesake. It seemed almost innocent, a peaceful bump on the horizon. But the SEALs often pointed to it and said, "That's the edge of the world. Beyond that? Chaos."

I'd chuckle, pretending it was just another joke. But deep down, I understood what they meant. Turtle Island wasn't just a piece of land—it was a reminder of how close we were to the border of Cambodia and the shadowy trails of the Ho Chi Minh supply line.

It was a constant, unspoken warning: Stay alert or you won't stay at all.

***

At first, I didn't belong at Roc Soi. Most of the boats had transitioned to Vietnamese crews, leaving the Americans in supporting roles like base defense. I wasn't a SEAL or a combat vet; I was just a guy trying to keep his head down. But that changed when the chow hall chef lost his baker.

"I need someone to bake bread," the chef announced one morning, barging into our barracks. "Anyone here know how?"

I didn't wait to hear if anyone else volunteered. "I can do it," I said, raising my hand.

The truth was, I'd never baked a damn thing in my life. But anything was better than throwing grenades into the river or standing watch in the sweltering towers. The chef didn't seem to care about my lack of experience.

"Good," he said. "No bad habits to unlearn."

The work was tough—kneading dough by hand, shaping loaves, and baking them through the night—but I found a strange solace in it. Something was rewarding about the process. Creating something tangible amidst the ambiguity. And it didn't hurt that it gave me an excuse to stay out of the heat during the day.

The SEALs, however, were the unexpected bonus. In the rigid military hierarchy, they existed on a plane all their own—a tight bond created by their impossible missions. Stories about them traveled across every base: their ability to swim miles underwater without breaking the surface, their uncanny skill in moving through jungle-like shadows, and their mental toughness that bordered on superhuman. Where the rest of us were trained to survive, the SEALs were trained to excel under conditions that would crush the average soldier.

Their rule was simple: No matter what time of day or night they returned from a mission, the chow hall stopped everything to feed them. They didn't need to ask, and they didn't wait in line. You knew when they entered the room—the air shifted, their presence filling every corner without a single word spoken.

At first, they were just faces in the crowd, shadowy figures who moved with a quiet confidence I could only hope to emulate. I was Navy, sure, but my job involved keeping engines running and baking bread—not navigating pitch-black swamps or dodging bullets deep in enemy territory. The SEALs, by comparison, seemed untouchable, almost mythical.

And yet, it was bread that broke the ice. One night, I set a tray of freshly baked loaves on the counter, their golden crusts still warm from the oven. One of the SEALs, a man with sharp eyes and a perpetual five o'clock shadow, stopped in his tracks.

"You make this?" he asked, his voice low but steady, the kind of tone that made you listen.

"Yeah," I replied, wiping my hands on my apron and suddenly feeling self-conscious. "First try."

He tore off a piece, inspecting it like it held some secret, then popped it into his mouth. He chewed slowly, his expression unreadable, before nodding.

"Not bad for a rookie."

That was it. No grand gesture, no speech. Just a nod of approval that felt like being knighted. From that moment, they weren't just SEALs anymore—they were people. And somehow, I had found a place in their orbit.

That was the beginning. Over time, they started calling me by name—or rather, by my last name, Burke. A few even invited me into their barracks, a privilege that came with unspoken rules. You didn't go into a SEAL's barracks uninvited. Ever.

***

The day before the town ambush, one of the SEALs cornered me in the chow hall.

"Burke," he said, leaning against the counter. "I hear you've been sneaking off to town to see the ladies."

I froze, my mind racing. "How the hell you know that?"

He smirked. "I know things."

"Well," I said, trying to keep my tone light, "I can't deny it."

"Take me with you," he said, his voice suddenly serious.

I stared at him. "You're joking, right?"

"Do I look like I'm joking?" He crossed his arms, his stance leaving no room for argument. "Tomorrow. I'm off. Don't make me ask twice."

The next day, I borrowed time off from the chef, and we headed into town. The SEAL was fluent in Vietnamese—a skill honed from countless missions in the jungle. I, on the other hand, could barely string together a curse word.

We rode in a Cushman, the three-wheeled-looking golf cart taxing us along the dirt road toward the city. Endless rice paddies surrounded us on both sides.

Halfway there, the driver slowed down. Too much.

"What's he doing?" I whispered.

The SEAL didn't answer. Instead, he pulled his sidearm and pressed it against the back of the driver's head.

In Vietnamese, he growled, "If you don't keep moving, I'll kill you here and now."

The driver stammered something, his hands trembling on the wheel.

Whatever he said, it didn't matter. The SEAL jabbed the gun forward. "Move. I might just kill you anyway, throw you out, and we'll take your Cushman."

The Cushman lurched forward, its engine whining as we sped down the road. We made it to town without incident, but the SEAL's warning stayed with me. The closer you stood to danger, the more the rules changed.

After surviving what could've been a deadly ambush, we agreed we needed to get to safety right away.

The SEAL nudged me toward the road. "Army barracks. Let's go."

We reached the barracks without incident. He walked in first, his posture calm but commanding. "I'm a Navy SEAL," he said, his tone leaving no room for argument. "We need a place to stay for the night."

The guard barely hesitated before nodding. "There are some bunks in the back. You're good to go."

The SEAL didn't introduce me or offer an explanation, and I didn't dare interject. Clearly, his status carried weight, even in the middle of nowhere.

The soldiers inside didn't ask questions. They pointed us to a couple of bunks in the corner, and we collapsed onto them without a word. The adrenaline finally started to wear off, leaving me feeling drained and hollow.

Inside, the barracks were sparse—metal-framed bunks, thin mattresses, and not much else. We each claimed a bed, and the SEAL cleaned his weapon, methodical and silent. I sat on the edge of my bunk, trying to process everything. The silence between us was heavy, filled with the unspoken realization that we'd barely made it out alive.

Finally, he glanced over at me, his face unreadable. "Burke, next time you want to bring bad luck along, leave me out of it."

I blinked, caught off guard. "Me? I wasn't the target."

Shaking his head, he firmly stated, "Doesn't matter."

I tried to laugh it off, but his words lingered. We both knew the truth: It wasn't my presence that had drawn the ambush—it was his status, his reputation. SEALs were the elite, high-value targets in every sense. One SEAL can easily take out 30 people. That's their capability, and the enemy knew that. Yet somehow, I still felt the pressure of it all.

Then, the near ambush in our room happened. The shuffling above us, the eerie silence that told us everything we needed to know, and the breath-taking escape back to the main road and away from the deathtrap that had been our room.

We climbed into another Cushman, the engine sputtering as it carried us away from the barracks and back toward the base. The ride was quiet, the adrenaline long gone, replaced by a bone-deep exhaustion. Neither of us said much. What was there to say?

When we reached the gates of Roc Soi, the SEAL stopped abruptly and turned to me.

"Burke, I'm never going to town with you again. You're a bad influence."

I stared at him, dumbfounded. "Wait a minute. I'm not the one they were after!"

He didn't reply, just shook his head and walked off, leaving me standing there. I watched him go, a mix of frustration and something else I couldn't quite name settling in my chest. For all his training and the danger he faced, he still carried himself like none of it could touch him. I envied that.

In a place like Roc Soi, survival wasn't just about skill. It was about finding moments of normalcy in a place that was far from the norm. And that's exactly what I set out to do.

***

One quiet night in the chow hall, I decided to push my luck. Baking bread had become second nature, and I was itching to try something new.

"Chef," I said, leaning on the counter, "what do you think about making donuts?"

The chef raised an eyebrow and let out a short laugh. "Donuts? Not a chance, Burke. We don't have the dough for that—donuts need something different."

I was ready to give up when he paused, rubbing his chin thoughtfully. "But," he said, "we could try cinnamon rolls. It's just bread dough sweetened up, and we've got cinnamon and sugar."

"Cinnamon rolls?" I repeated, my curiosity piqued.

He nodded. "Yeah. You roll the dough out, sprinkle on the cinnamon and sugar, twist it, and bake it. We even have enough sugar to make a glaze, which is rare out here."

It didn't take much convincing. Within minutes, I was elbow-deep in flour, kneading the dough and rolling it out nice and thin. I spread the cinnamon and sugar mixture over the surface, twisting the dough into tight spirals before setting them on the trays to rise.

By the time the first tray was ready for the oven, the warm, sugary scent started to fill the air. The smell made you forget where you were, if only for a moment.

The next few hours flew by in a haze of flour, sugar, and cinnamon. I rolled out the dough, sprinkled on the cinnamon and sugar, and twisted it into tight spirals. The makeshift oven hissed and hummed as I baked two massive trays, each 30 by 30, packed with cinnamon rolls. The warm, sugary scent filled the kitchen, spilling out into the base like a sweet beacon cutting through the war zone.

It was near midnight when the first tray was ready—I was eager to have the sweet treat prepared for the morning. I'd barely set it on the counter when the door swung open, and a familiar figure walked in.

The SEAL—my SEAL—stopped in his tracks, his nose twitching as the smell hit him. Behind him, the rest of his team filed in like a row of dominos, their movements sharp and deliberate, almost colliding into him since the SEAL put his brakes on without notice.

"Burke, what the fuck did you bake?" he asked, his voice breaking the silence.

"It's just bread, man," I replied.

He looks me straight in the eye and remarked, "No, that is not bread I'm smelling."

"Well, I baked these," setting the tray down with a grin.

He approached the counter cautiously, like a soldier inspecting enemy territory. "Cinnamon rolls," his tone skeptical. "In Vietnam?"

"Fresh out of the oven," I said, holding back a laugh. "Try one."

The first bite was hesitant, almost experimental. But then his face broke into a rare smile that softened his sharp edges. Without another word, he grabbed another roll, and the rest of the SEALs followed suit, devouring the tray before I could set the second one down. Their faces lit up like kids on Christmas morning.

It wasn't long before they'd gone through both trays, leaving only a few sticky crumbs and the scent of cinnamon in the air—all before they even touched their dinner.

The cinnamon rolls didn't just disappear; they disappeared with an intensity that only men in the field, deprived of small comforts, could muster.

One of the SEALs leaned back, satisfied, and muttered, "Haven't had anything like this since I landed in this damn place."

A lieutenant—though you wouldn't know it by looking at him—approached me. SEALs didn't wear rank insignias; they blended in by design. Their lieutenants weren't the kind to hang back or stick to protocol. They could just as easily be at the front of the pack as the rear.

He came right up to me and said, "From now on, when we go out, we'll let you know. That's not something we usually do." He paused, a faint grin on his face.

"But when we get back, I want to see cinnamon rolls sitting on that counter."

I nodded, the significance of his words settling in. "I can do that."

It was a quiet exchange, but it impacted me. In a place where survival often hinged on who you trusted, this felt like a turning point.

***

Life on the base moved in rhythms dictated by necessity. One morning, I found myself in personnel, asking for a reassignment. My current post was a Temporary Assigned Duty—TAD, they called it—and I figured it was time to move on. I really missed working as a mechanic on American boats.

"I'd like to be reassigned," I told the clerk, a middle-aged man who looked like he hadn't slept in weeks.

He nodded, barely looking up. "We'll work on it," he said, his tone noncommittal. "We'll let you know."

I left the office with no idea where I might end up. Maps of Vietnam weren't exactly handed out to guys like me. I could be sent somewhere far worse for all I knew. Either way, it wasn't up to me.

***

In the meantime, supplies were running low, and a trip to the Binh Thuy base was on the schedule. Binh Thuy was a hub—a sprawling expanse with airfields, storage depots, and rows of PBRs docked in neat lines. If we needed it, Binh Thuy had it.

Our crew of six loaded into a big blue and white Navy truck, armed and ready for anything. The route was long, winding through villages and rice paddies, and there were no guarantees about who controlled what. The possibility of an ambush loomed over every mile.

As we approached the convoy's staging area, the chef stepped up, his demeanor as casual as ever despite the tension in the air. "Mind if I tag along?" he asked, addressing the officer in charge of our truck.

The officer hesitated. "What's a chef doing on a supply run?"

"Making sure you all get fed," the chef quipped. "And maybe making sure you don't get yourselves killed on the way back."

The officer shrugged. "Suit yourself. Just don't get in the way."

And with that, the chef climbed aboard, settling into the front passenger seat. His presence was oddly reassuring—like having someone who could turn the worst day into a half-decent one with a quick joke or a good meal.

***

The trip started uneventfully, with our truck trailing an Army convoy for added security. But just as we passed through a small village, the lead truck screeched to a halt, and the unmistakable sound of a .50 caliber machine gun rang out.

"They've got the lead truck," someone muttered, panic creeping into their voice.

I craned my neck, catching sight of the disabled vehicle riddled with bullet holes. The driver and passenger were down, and the convoy froze.

Then, like clockwork, the Army tanks sprang into action. One tank veered left, the other right, their massive cannons swiveling toward the source of the gunfire.

"Hold on," I whispered to myself as the tanks unleashed hell.

The village ahead erupted in a cacophony of explosions, the sheer force rattling the ground beneath us. Armored personnel carriers (APCs) flanked the tanks, their doors swinging open as soldiers poured out to secure the perimeter.

"They're not taking chances," someone said beside me, their voice tight with both awe and fear.

When the smoke cleared, the convoy regrouped. We stayed at the back, our truck a modest shadow compared to the behemoths that had just saved us. As we rolled through the wreckage, an officer came down the line, barking orders.

"Do not stop for anything," he said. "Run over whatever's in the road. Keep moving."

And that's exactly what we did. Through villages and towns—anything that didn't move fast enough was flattened. The tanks led the way, constantly reminding us of what could happen if we hesitated.

***

By the time we reached Binh Thuy, the tension was palpable. We loaded the supplies quickly, knowing the return trip would be even riskier. There was no convoy to follow this time—just us, a lone Navy truck with a skeleton crew.

We drove fast, and every shadow along the road was a potential threat. My knuckles were white as I gripped my weapon, scanning the horizon for any sign of movement. But somehow, we made it back to Roc Soi unscathed.

As I stepped off the truck, my legs shaky from the adrenaline, I couldn't help but think of the destroyed village, the lead truck rid-

He gave me a look; the kind that told me I was about to learn the hard way.

dled with bullets, and the tanks that had saved the day. Without them, we might not have made it out alive.

***

Not long after that, my reassignment orders came through. I unfolded the paper, scanning the unfamiliar name: Nam Can Solid Anchor.

Clutching the slip, I made my way to one of the SEALs—a guy I trusted more than most, someone who had earned his reputation through grit and quiet wisdom.

"You know where this is?" I asked, holding out the paper. I laughed nervously, trying to brush off the knot forming in my stomach. "Well, I guess I'm about to find out. Why do you think the captain's sending me there?"

He hesitated, his lips pressing into a thin line. "We don't trust him and he knows it," he said finally, the weight of his words hanging in the air. "And if he's sending you to Nam Can, it's not out of the goodness of his heart."

I blinked. "What's that supposed to mean?"

The SEAL's eyes flickered toward the ground, then back to me. "He doesn't like us. Never has. We don't let him into the barracks. Seems he doesn't like you either. There's no proof, but..." He trailed off, lowering his voice. "Some of us think he's too close with the South Vietnamese leadership. Too close for comfort."

I folded the paper back into my pocket, the knot in my stomach tightening. Nam Can. The name carried weight now, more than just a place on a map. It was a destination shaped by suspicion and isolation.

One of the most remote postings in Vietnam, it was 190 miles south of Saigon, accessible only by helicopter. If Roc Soi was challenging, Nam Can felt like a leap into the unknown.

As I packed my gear, I couldn't shake the SEAL's words. I'd survived rockets on the river, ambushes in alleys, and chaotic supply runs, but something about this felt different. It wasn't just the place—it was the intention behind it. I was being sent there for a reason, and it wasn't because anyone thought I'd enjoy the scenery.

I couldn't help but wonder: *What had I gotten myself into this time?*

CHAPTER 4

No Roads, No Retreat

If the jungle doesn't kill me, this place might.

The thought hit me as I stood on the tarmac, staring at the olive-green helicopter descending, its double rotors slicing through the humid air. The roar of the blades was deafening, vibrating through my chest, but the weight of what lay ahead pressed down harder.

This wasn't a plane, the kind I'd expected for a base transfer. This was a Jolly Green Giant—a machine built for rugged missions, not casual commutes.

The SEAL's words from a few days ago echoed in my mind.

"You'll find out," he'd said, his tone even but his expression grim. It wasn't like him to hold back, but he'd said just enough to let me know I wasn't heading to paradise.

"Why a Jolly Green?" I muttered to myself as I stepped toward the helicopter. A crewman waved me forward, his face obscured by goggles and a helmet.

The Jolly Green Giant wasn't exactly a new piece of machinery. It was an old workhorse designed to haul troops and equipment. It was functional and reliable, but not the kind of ride you'd expect for a short hop between bases. The stale smell of oil and metal filled my nostrils as I climbed aboard. The seats were rough, the straps frayed, and the windows streaked with grime.

I buckled in and glanced out the window as the helicopter lifted off.

The helicopter's blades roared, the vibrations rattling through my boots. The floating barracks of Roc Soi shrank below me, rice paddies and villages blending into a patchwork quilt of green and brown. The heaviness of the slip in my pocket pressed against me, a reminder of the unknown ahead.

For the first half of the flight, I could make out the narrow roads snaking through the countryside and the occasional glint of water. But as we flew further south, the terrain changed. The roads disappeared, swallowed by dense jungle that stretched as far as I could see. Rivers, hidden beneath the thick canopy, were mere hints of blue veins.

The knot in my stomach tightened. This wasn't just remote—this was the edge of nowhere.

I looked around the cabin, hoping for some reassurance. The crew, busy with their instruments, paid me no mind. I shifted uncomfortably, the enormity of the jungle stretching endlessly below as I stared out the window.

By the time we landed, soaked in sweat, the helicopter's jarring thud revealed a base barely worthy of being called a base. There were no paved roads, no bustling activity—just a cluster of buildings surrounded by jungle and water.

As I stepped off the ramp, duffel bag in hand, the heat hit me like a wall. The air was almost syrupy and smelled of rot and stagnant water.

My boots resonated off of the metal landing platform.

"I'm in it now," I muttered, surveying my new home.

The isolation was immediate and complete. There were no roads leading in or out, no bustling market or corner bar to escape to. The jungle loomed on all sides, an impenetrable wall of green that seemed to press closer with every second, its dense canopy cutting off any hint of sky. The air inside carried a damp, earthy smell that clung to my skin. It wasn't just the physical presence—it was a feeling of being watched, as if the jungle itself was alive, waiting for a moment of weakness to close in. The only connection to the outside world was the helicopter that had brought me here.

A soldier approached me, his uniform stained and his face weary.

"Welcome to Nam Can," he said, his voice flat. "Couple of things you'll want to know. First, don't drink the water unless it's mixed with Kool-Aid."

I frowned. "Why not?"

He smirked but didn't elaborate. "You'll figure it out."

Later, I would. The "water" came straight from wells drilled into the swamp, saturated with Agent Orange and other toxic chemicals. It wasn't just the taste—the long-term effects of drinking it concerned everyone. The Kool-Aid didn't purify it—it just masked the taste of the chemical cocktail we were forced to drink.

***

That first day, they put me on base defense. Apart from the defoliated section about a quarter mile out, Nam Cam didn't have a proper perimeter. No barbed wire. No claymores. The jungle crept right up to the edge of the base as if daring us to cross the invisible boundary. My job? Stringing wire through the swamp to create a makeshift barrier.

I'd cut the legs off an old pair of fatigues to deal with the heat, but it wasn't enough. The swamp water was warm and slimy, and within minutes, I felt the first leech latch onto my leg. By the time I waded out, I was covered in them.

One of the other guys saw me and shook his head. "You can't just pull 'em off," he said, tossing me a lit cigarette. "Burn 'em."

The leeches didn't just suck blood—they left behind whatever was in the water. And in Nam Can, that meant a little bit of poison with every bite.

When I wasn't in the swamp, I stood watch in one of the three towers facing the jungle. We had night-vision scopes, but they were clunky—two feet long and big as a coffee can around…and about just as helpful.

While scanning the tree line one night, I saw a flashlight beam flicker on and off. It moved methodically, too deliberate to be anything but a person.

I called it into the main control tower. "There's someone at the tree line," I said, my voice low.

The reply crackled back a moment later, rousing the Marine officer in charge from his quarters. It was late—sometime between midnight and 2 a.m., though I didn't have a watch to check. Within minutes, he was climbing into the tower, his face etched with sleep-deprived irritation.

We'd just finished smoking a little marijuana. Fortunately, being out in the open, the breeze carried away the last traces of smoke just before the officer reached the top of the watchtower.

"What are you looking at?" the officer grumbled, leaning toward the clunky scope I'd been using.

I pointed toward the tree line. "Right there, sir."

"How long has it been there?" he asked, adjusting the scope.

"Not sure. Just noticed it."

He didn't waste time. "Is the .50 loaded?"

"Always," I replied.

"Shoot it."

The .50 caliber roared to life, its thunderous firepower vibrating through my body as I squeezed the trigger. Capable of shooting up to two miles, the gun's magnitude was staggering. The recoil shook the tower with each shot, sending me swaying as I fought to steady the barrel.

The rounds tore through the jungle, shredding foliage and lighting up the night. By contrast, the lighter M60 could have been used, but the officer wanted to make a point with this shot, and the .50 left no room for ambiguity.

The light disappeared.

"Think you got it," the officer said, his tone clipped. "Next time, don't wait for me. You see something, you shoot it."

His words hung in the air as he climbed back down, leaving me alone with the smoldering barrel of the .50 and the echoes of gunfire still ringing in my ears.

Standing in that swaying watchtower, my hands still tingling from gripping the .50 caliber, I understood the unspoken rule of Nam Can: Hesitation could get you killed. From that night forward, if I saw a shadow flicker or a flashlight beam cut through the dense jungle, I didn't hesitate.

***

The next rotation brought a new assignment, and I couldn't have been more relieved. With its murky water, leeches, and the toxic cocktail of diesel and Agent Orange, the swamp was no longer my concern. The mortar pit was losing a few men, rotating out of the base, and the lieutenant needed replacements.

It happened quickly. The lieutenant stormed into the barracks one humid afternoon, his voice cutting through the stagnant air like a whip.

"I need volunteers for the mortar team!" he barked.

I didn't wait. I was out of the cubicle before he finished his sentence, my boots hitting the floor with purpose. Reichel, another guy from my barracks, followed closely behind. The thought of standing another watch in the towers or wading back into the swamp made the mortar pit's danger seem almost appealing.

The lieutenant's eyes swept over us as we lined up. "You sure about this?"

"Yes, sir," I said, my voice steady.

The mortar pit had its own rhythm, a deadly cadence of preparation and precision. When we arrived, we were introduced to the departing crew, a couple of Californians who looked more like surfers than soldiers. Dressed in Levi's and t-shirts, they defied every military stereotype.

"Mosquitoes can't bite through denim," one of them said with a shrug when I asked about their attire. "And leeches? Pantyhose under the Levi's. Works like a charm."

I didn't argue. After my first encounter with the swamp, I'd believe anything.

Then came the gunnery sergeant—a black Marine with a presence that could fill the entire pit. He was unlike anyone I'd ever met, equal parts brilliance and eccentricity.

"You ever shot a mortar?" he asked, his sharp gaze locking onto me.

"No, sir."

He looked around at the other recruits, their heads shaking in unison. Then he turned back to me. "What would you do?"

I didn't hesitate. Picking up two mortar rounds, one in each hand, I walked to the tube and dropped them rapidly. The first round launched with a deafening whoosh, and before its echo faded, the second followed. The sergeant's grin widened with every thump.

"Can you keep doing that?" he asked.

"If it keeps me alive, yes, sir," I said, straightening up.

"Good," he replied, clapping a hand on my shoulder. "Because that's your job now."

That's how I met Carl, the guy who would become my closest ally on the mortar team. Carl was no-nonsense, the kind of guy who didn't waste words but carried an air of quiet confidence. He'd been on the team longer, and he knew the ropes. Our bond solidified quickly, especially after I saw him survive near-death during a mortar attack.

It happened one night while Carl was running from the barracks to the bunker. A Vietnamese kid, leaning casually against the bunker, laughed as Carl passed. Moments later, a mortar landed, obliterating the spot where the kid had been standing. Carl hit the ground unscathed as shrapnel sprayed in every direction, missing him entirely.

"You've got a guardian angel," I told him later, only half-joking.

From that moment, I stayed as close to Carl as I could. If I could have looped my belt to his, I would have. Carl wanted me on the team because of how I shot—methodical, relentless, and precise. And I wanted to be near him because, somehow, he seemed untouchable.

The mortar pit became my world. Each night, from dusk till dawn, we launched harassment fire into the jungle as we targeted suspected enemy positions. The mortars' range extended three miles, and we used every bit of it. We'd start at maximum range, then work our way closer, adjusting the angle and direction to keep the enemy guessing where we'd fire next.

***

The SEALs became even closer allies during this time. They'd taken a liking to our team and decided to show us exactly where the mortars were coming from. One night, they guided us down the river and through the dense, triple-canopy jungle to scout enemy positions.

The SEALs led the way, their movements deliberate and quiet. Carl, however, stood out like a walking arsenal. He had grenades strapped to his vest, ammunition slung across his chest, a knife in his boot, and his trusty M16 cradled in his arms. The man looked ready to take on the entire Viet Cong by himself.

"Why so much gear?" I asked, raising an eyebrow.

Carl grinned, adjusting his bandolier. "Because I'm not planning to die unarmed. You should try it sometime."

I chuckled, shaking my head as I checked my equipment—a single M16 and a few spare magazines.

Carl was never one to back down, but sometimes his confidence led to moments like this. As our PBR swung in toward the shore, Carl, armed to the teeth, decided he didn't need to wait for a proper landing. "The river can't be that deep," he muttered, more to himself than anyone else. Before anyone could stop him, he leapt off the back of the boat.

It was deeper than he expected—far deeper. He sank like a rock, the weight of his gear pulling him straight to the bottom. The river's dark, murky water swallowed him whole. The SEALs and I stood on the shore, watching and waiting. The seconds dragged on.

One of the SEALs leaned toward me, his voice low. "If he's not up in 20 seconds, I'm going in after him."

I nodded; my eyes fixed on the spot where Carl had disappeared. And then, just as panic started to creep in, he emerged. Knees bent, he launched himself up from the bottom with one powerful push. Breaking through the surface, he spit out a mouthful of water, took a deep breath, and grabbed his floating hat. He jammed it back on his head and trudged out of the river without missing a beat.

Not a single piece of his equipment was missing. His grenades, his ammunition, his M16—everything was intact. Carl, soaked but utterly unfazed, looked every bit the unstoppable force he wanted to be.

"Why the hell did you do that?" I asked, incredulous.

Carl shrugged; his grin as casual as if he'd just walked out of a warm shower. "I'm not going to be unarmed," he said. "You might be, but I'm not."

The SEALs and I stifled our laughter, conscious of how sound carried in the jungle. But the image of Carl, soaked to the bone but still clinging to every piece of his arsenal, was almost too much to handle.

After that, we moved into the jungle. The jungle was relentless. As soon as we stepped five feet into its dense embrace, the river behind us vanished. It was like the water had never existed. One moment, you were standing on the shoreline, and the next, you were swallowed whole by the green. It was almost surreal—how the thick vegetation closed in around you. The jungle had already erased our path.

Voices carried in the jungle, and the last thing we needed was to announce our presence to anyone listening.

The trek was grueling. The ground was soft and uneven, the kind that sucked at your boots with every step. Sweat poured down my face, stinging my eyes, and the air felt like I was breathing through a wet rag. The jungle was alive with sound—birds squawking, insects buzzing, and the occasional rustle of something larger moving through the underbrush. But we didn't speak. Voices carried in the jungle, and the last thing we needed was to announce our presence to anyone listening.

After what felt like an eternity, the jungle opened up into a small clearing. The SEAL leading the group raised his hand, signaling us to stop. He crouched low, his sharp eyes scanning the area before motioning us forward.

"This is one of the spots," he whispered, his voice barely audible. "They've been shooting at you from here."

I stepped closer, my eyes following his pointing finger. The ground had been cleared just enough to set up a mortar. The vegetation was chopped back to provide a direct line of sight to the base. It was unsettling to see how calculated the setup was—how the enemy had turned this peaceful clearing into a launchpad for destruction.

"How far out are we?" Carl asked, his tone all business.

"About three miles from the base," the SEAL replied. "They're smart. They know how to stay just out of your range."

Carl nodded, his grip tightening on his M16. "Figures."

The SEALs led us to a second site, this one even closer to the base. It was west of the first location, near what we called "the road." The ground here was littered with remnants of past battles—shell casings, bits of metal, and scorched patches of earth—a grim reminder of how persistent the enemy was.

"They've got this place dialed in," the SEAL said, his face grim. "They use these spots to harass you, but they're careful. As soon as you fire back, they're gone."

Carl glanced at me, his expression unreadable. "They're not stupid. They know what they're doing."

As we sat back at the base that night, the reality of what we'd seen settled over us. The mortar positions weren't random—they were strategic, designed to chip away at our morale and resources. Knowing the enemy could strike and disappear before we had a chance to retaliate was frustrating.

***

Life on the base was monotonous. The same routines, the same faces, the same gnawing sense of unease that came with being in a war zone. To break the monotony, we'd found a jeep left behind, turning it into our makeshift escape. We'd race down the runway, laughing like kids as we kicked up clouds of dust, our guns slung across our backs. It wasn't much, but it was something.

The base itself had changed during our time there. It was no longer called Nam Can but Truong Hung Dao 4, reflecting the transition to Vietnamese control. With the Americans in the minority, we felt the shift in dynamics. The SEALs, who had become our closest allies, warned us to be cautious. Trust was a scarce commodity, even among supposed allies.

One of our biggest challenges was ammunition. We fired so many rounds nightly that we couldn't risk calling in orders—they'd be intercepted. Instead, Carl and I were often sent to Saigon to secure what we needed. The trips were long and dangerous, but they were necessary. Without those runs, we'd be sitting ducks.

The ammunition runs were always an ordeal. Carl and I took turns, our trips to Saigon punctuated by moments that teetered between absurdity and sheer terror. Carl's previous trip was a perfect example: He'd boarded a Huey helicopter for the ride, a mode of transport that offered no seatbelts and plenty of ways to fall out. Mid-flight, the pilot made a sharp maneuver, throwing Carl against the edge of the open doorway. His fingernails were the only thing keeping him from plummeting to the ground below. He pulled himself back in by some miracle, his heart pounding but his grip on life intact.

When it was my turn, I boarded an Army helicopter—a rarity given our location. The pilot and crew were already lounging as if they'd been waiting for an excuse to fly. Lopez, the guy who handled transportation on our base, flagged them down, asking if they could give me a lift.

"Where to?" the crew chief asked, lazily chewing on a piece of gum.

"Saigon," Lopez replied.

The crewman shrugged. "Yeah, sure. We're heading that way anyway."

I climbed aboard and quickly noticed something unusual about this helicopter. The door gunner, stationed on one side, was equipped with a minigun—a recent upgrade. He handed me a headset, but I could only hear him, not the pilots. As I settled in, my gaze dropped to the floor, where small holes dotted the metal beneath my boots.

"Ventilation?" I asked the gunner, gesturing to the holes.

He smirked. "Nah, that's from getting shot at from below."

With that unsettling revelation, I placed my helmet on the seat—not for safety, but to sit on. If they were shooting up at us, I wanted some protection for my manhood.

***

The flight took us above the clouds, offering a temporary reprieve from the oppressive jungle below. The view was breathtaking, but it came with a bitter edge.

"Why so high?" I asked the gunner.

"Short-timers," he said, nodding toward the pilots. "Between the three of us, we've got three and a half months left in-country. Staying high keeps us out of range."

The casual nature of their risk avoidance was almost amusing. These guys weren't on a mission; they were killing time, trying to avoid trouble. Or so I thought.

Halfway through the flight, the door gunner pulled out a joint and lit it. He held it up to me, eyebrows raised in invitation.

"Why not?" I said, taking a drag. When he gestured to the front, I shook my head.

"Oh, they'll take it," he assured me.

I knelt between the two pilots, holding up the joint. One took it, inhaled deeply, then passed it to the other. It struck me then that I was flying with four stoned men in a Huey helicopter. The absurdity of it all hit me hard, but before I could laugh, the vibe shifted.

***

One of the pilots banged his armrest, snapping everyone to attention. The gunner leaned toward me. "We've been called into a firefight. Army convoy's under attack."

All traces of the mellowed-out crew vanished. The Huey dropped out of the clouds, descending rapidly toward the chaos below. The village came into view, and the pilots wasted no time.

As we banked left, the door gunner nudged me, pulling me out of focus. "Hey," he shouted over the roar of the helicopter, "when we land, stick close to me. It's gonna get hairy." I nodded, gripping the tether of my M60 as if my life depended on it—which it did.

The ground below erupted as the Huey's rockets hit their targets, shaking the helicopter so hard it felt like the entire craft might shatter midair. The turmoil wasn't contained to the village. Smoke billowed in every direction, and the enemy fire approached us in sporadic bursts.

As we circled for another run, I caught sight of the convoy pinned down. Army soldiers scrambled for cover, firing back as best they could. My heart pounded as the pilot angled the Huey sharply, lining up another volley of rockets. The door gunner started firing his minigun in rhythmic bursts, the spent casings raining down into the jungle.

Through the windshield, I watched as the rockets found their marks, the village erupting in flames and debris. The Huey banked left, circling the village while the door gunner opened fire. The sound was deafening, a relentless roar as spent shells rained down like metallic hail.

"Your turn," the gunner shouted, motioning toward the M60 on my side.

I grabbed the weapon and aimed at the madness below. The recoil hit me hard, the tethered gun jerking in my hands as the helicopter swayed. My shots felt random and scattered, but the gunner nodded approvingly.

We circled once more, releasing another barrage of rockets before pulling away. The convoy on the ground signaled that the threat had been neutralized. With that, we climbed back above the clouds, the adrenaline fading as quickly as it had spiked.

***

We made an unplanned stop at a small Army outpost for fuel. It was nothing more than a few tents and barbed wire, but it served its purpose. As we refueled, the door gunner turned to me.

"When we get to Saigon, you wanna grab a drink?" he asked.

"Sure," I said. "Why not?"

When we finally landed at Tân Sơn Nhứt Air Base, it was a sprawling maze of aircraft and activity.

"Looks like our ride's waiting for us," the door gunner joked as we spotted an unmarked Jeep near the airstrip.

I raised an eyebrow. "We just… take it?"

"That's the idea," he said, hopping into the driver's seat without hesitation.

The Jeep didn't have flags or markings, but the keys were in the ignition, practically inviting us to commandeer it. As we approached the gate, the guards didn't ask questions. They saluted, and we drove out into the streets of Saigon like we owned the place, assuming we were officers.

We drove into Saigon without incident, parking haphazardly outside a bar. Inside, we laughed and shared drinks, the tension of the day melting away. When I left, the Jeep was gone—probably stolen by someone else. It was just another day in Vietnam.

The next morning, I handled my business. It was time to secure the ammunition we needed before hitching a ride back to Nam Can. My mind was already on the next steps to secure the ammunition, so I walked down the street wearing my tiger jungle greens. Those weren't just any uniform—they were special issue, reserved for particular units or those stationed in areas like Nam Can. I'd been authorized to wear them, but it still drew attention.

A short military police Jeep pulled onto the sidewalk in front of me. Two MPs jumped out, one clearly agitated. He pointed at my uniform.

"Why are you wearing those?" he demanded, his tone sharp.

Before I could respond, the other officer stepped forward and took a calmer approach. "Let's see your orders," he said, holding out his hand.

I reached into my pocket and handed them over, my face unreadable. As he scanned the papers, the first officer continued questioning me, his voice growing more aggressive.

The calmer MP finally spoke up. "Hold it. He's Navy and assigned to Nam Can," he said, a hint of respect in his voice. "He's authorized to wear those and carry that .45. Let it go."

The first officer's demeanor shifted instantly. He handed back my orders with a muttered apology, and they drove off, leaving me to wonder if I'd face this same interrogation every time I set foot in Saigon.

***

Not even a block later, another Jeep pulled up beside me, this time the Navy Shore Patrol. Two sailors hopped out, one with the same accusing tone as before.

"Let me see your papers," he barked.

I sighed, pulling out my orders for the second time in less than ten minutes. The other sailor grabbed them, his eyes scanning the document carefully.

The calmer sailor smirked and turned to his partner. "Leave him alone," he said. "He just walked out of the jungle, and he might shoot your ass if you keep this up."

He handed me back my papers with a grin. "Carry on," he added.

I didn't wait to see if another Jeep would stop me this time. I hailed a taxi and decided to avoid walking altogether. I'd had enough of being questioned for one day.

Although the return trip was uneventful compared to the trip to Saigon, the urgency of our mission stayed with me. Every round we brought back meant another night of holding the line, another chance to survive.

Before I could return to the mortar pit, Carl pulled me aside with a mischievous grin. "We got a present," he said, leading me to the corner of the CONEX box—the shipping container we used for storage.

Tucked behind a stack of flare rounds was a burlap sack. Carl tugged it open, revealing a tightly packed bale of marijuana.

"Courtesy of the California guys before they left," he explained. "Figured we'd need this more than beer out here."

We laughed, but the gesture was more meaningful than it seemed. In a place where survival meant finding small comforts in the madness, this was a reminder that camaraderie stretched beyond the front lines.

The rhythm of war was relentless, but in those small moments—flying above the clouds, sharing a laugh with strangers—we found ways to carry on. It wasn't about winning or losing. It was about getting through one more day.

***

The decision to visit the fishing village down the river seemed harmless at first. Carl and I, along with a Vietnamese Navy officer and another sailor, took the trip out of sheer curiosity—and, perhaps, boredom. The officer had agreed to come along, knowing we couldn't speak the language and would need someone to guide us.

When we arrived, the village appeared humble and quiet. Children, elderly men, and women, whose lives seemed untouched by the chaos that consumed much of Vietnam. The sand pans lining the river weren't large fishing vessels but modest, worn boats that could barely manage a day's catch.

Six teenagers emerged from the muddy gangplanks as we strolled through the village. They didn't stand out at first—just boys in everyday clothing—but something about their demeanor gave Carl pause. He stopped and asked to take their picture. They didn't object, standing stiffly as Carl framed the shot. The Vietnamese officer didn't share Carl's enthusiasm. He stood off to the side, his hands on his hips, glaring at the boys.

Afterward, the officer pulled us aside, his voice low and urgent. "Those are the ones shooting at you every night," he said. "They're Viet Cong, living in the village."

The Vietnamese officer's glare at the teenage boys gave a silent but clear message—we know who you are, and don't you dare try and pull anything.

Even still, the realization hit me like a mortar round. These weren't just kids hanging out in a village. They were the enemy.

Yet, dressed as civilians, they were untouchable. We couldn't arrest them or take any action without concrete evidence. It was a frustrating reminder of how blurred the lines were in this war.

When the boat failed to return to take us back to base, the officer arranged for us to stay overnight. The accommodations were as rustic as they come. One house had a pig sleeping under the bed, a sight that would've been amusing under different circumstances. That night, Carl, the officer, and I took turns standing guard, uneasy in the knowledge that those kids, the enemy, were just a stone's throw away. They had us on their own turf.

By morning, the boat arrived, and we returned to base with a sobering new perspective: The war wasn't just "out there" in the jungle. It was everywhere, even in the quietest of places.

Nam Can wasn't just a base—it was a test. Every leech, every shadow in the jungle, and every flicker of doubt hammered home the same truth: Survival here meant adapting quickly and leaving hesitation behind.

In this place, the only constant was that nothing stayed still—not the jungle, not the war, and not the man I was becoming. But even here, amidst the unpredictability, some moments reminded us we were human—moments of camaraderie, laughter, and ingenuity that made the war feel a little less heavy, even if only for a while.

CHAPTER 5

MORTARS, MONKEYS, AND MAYHEM

"The problem is, it's right in plain sight. Here's these, but you didn't get them from us."

The SEALs had a way of showing up just when things felt unbearable, not to lend a hand but to remind us that we could have some fun, too.

Life on the base had its fair share of challenges, not the least of which was the lack of refrigeration. Warm beer and soda were the norm, and even those were hard to come by. One evening, two SEALs stopped by our pit with a proposition.

"There's an extra fridge in a CONEX box by the NCO club," one of them said, referring to the Non-Commissioned Officer's Club, with a mischievous glint in his eye.

They handed us a pair of bolt cutters and left without another word. Carl, the other guys in the pit, and I created a plan. We'd fake an attack on the base to draw attention away from the area. Setting our mortars to fire almost vertically, we fabricated the illusion of incoming rounds.

The chaos gave us the cover we needed.

Dressed in black, Carl and I crept toward the road toward the CON-EX box, cut the lock, and hauled the refrigerator back to our hooch. Once inside our living space, we didn't bother hiding it; instead, we tucked it behind a curtain and plugged it in.

The next day, officers came searching for the missing fridge. One of them, a friend, volunteered to check our barracks. "It's not in here," he called out, winking as he stepped back outside. The search ended there.

Later, our officer stopped by. In a moment of sheer stupidity, I offered him a cold soda. His eyes narrowed as he took a sip. "This is good," he said, clearly aware of what it meant.

The officer lingered for a moment, his gaze lingering on the cold soda sweating in his hand. He chuckled lightly.

"You know," he said, leaning slightly against the table, "I could raise hell about this. But why would I? You boys are doing your jobs—keeping us all alive."

He paused, looking around the room. "I've seen bases where morale is shot to hell. That's not going to happen here, not on my watch. Besides," he grinned, raising the soda, "this is damn good. Keep it up."

It wasn't just an unspoken approval but an acknowledgment of what mattered most—getting through another day.

Amid the harshness of war, the small, ridiculous victories—like a cold soda or a clever heist—made base life bearable.

And then there was Baby, the monkey who managed to outshine all of us.

We found comfort in making it to the next day in the unlikeliest of companions: a squirrel monkey named Baby. Carl had adopted her early on, and she quickly became the mortar team's unofficial mascot. Small and feisty, Baby was a constant source of entertainment.

She clung to Carl like a child, following him everywhere. At night, she slept beneath his cot. During the day, she perched on his shoulder, surveying the world with curious eyes. Her antics were a welcome distraction from the monotony and danger of base life.

One day, a team from *Stars and Stripes* came to do a story on our mortar pit. We were ready to share our experiences, but Baby had other plans. The reporters couldn't get enough of her. By the time the article was published, it was all about Baby. Carl and I were footnotes, outshone by a monkey in our own story.

***

The South Vietnamese Army's plans often felt detached from reality, but their next move was something beyond what we could have predicted. Sometime before Christmas, they decided to launch an assault on the fortified North Vietnamese base to our south.

The SEALs, however, had made it clear to us early on: Don't shoot south.

"We're not getting attacked from there," one of the SEALs said firmly. "If you fire in that direction, you'll stir up a hornet's nest. There's a lot of them down there, and trust me, you don't want them heading north."

We listened. The mortar aimed south remained silent, collecting dust.

But one day, that all changed when a bunch of uppity-ups from the Vietnamese Army, our Army, and the Marines showed up to see how well we shot our mortars. They wanted to join together to lead an offensive. It was poorly planned from the start.

Before the attack, several officers gathered behind our mortar pit, standing on a platform initially used to distribute sand during the base's construction. With binoculars in hand, they picked random spots on the perimeter for us to target.

"That cluster of trees over there," one of them barked.

We knew the range by heart; it was where we practiced regularly. Reichel, manning the mortar, adjusted the sights. The first round was Willie Peter—a white phosphorus grenade known for its smoke and ability to leave a burn. It exploded at the base of the trees, sending up a thick beam of smoke.

"Fire for effect!" another officer shouted.

Reichel went to work, dropping round after round.

"Boom. Boom. Boom."

The trees vanished in a flurry of splinters and flame. Satisfied, the officers directed us to another spot, repeating the process. When they finally left, they seemed impressed.

"These guys are pretty good. I think they'll do."

A week later, the attack began. Helicopters ferried troops south while others arrived by boat. But their assault lacked coordination. There was no preparatory bombardment, no suppression fire—just soldiers marching into a death trap.

Our base's makeshift hospital turned into a triage center, with helicopters constantly bringing in the injured and dead. Carl and I stayed at our post, waiting for an order to fire south that never came. They were so uncoordinated with their attack that there was no way for us to shoot because we would've ended up shooting our own guys.

By midday, the operation had been abandoned. The fortified enemy base remained untouched, and the cost was high. The SEALs had been right all along.

The lack of coordination didn't just cost lives—it created a ripple effect that brought the harsh realities of war to our doorstep. The M.A.S.H. unit became a battlefield of its own, with medics working desperately to save the soldiers brought in by helicopter. As a mortar crew, we weren't trained for this, but that day, we became stretcher-bearers, orderlies, and whatever was needed to keep the system moving.

As helicopters transported the wounded back to base that day, I was asked to help unload the injured. At first, it was a blur of motion—shouting medics, the thrum of chopper blades, and the groans of men in pain.

Most of the wounded were walking or being helped along, but then a stretcher came off, and I froze. The man on it was eerily still, covered from the chest down by a blanket. As we carried him, the air from the helicopter blades caught the fabric and lifted it, revealing his legs—or what was left of them.

Both were gone, severed at the knees. For a moment, I couldn't move. The sight was burned into my mind. "Cover him back up," someone barked, jolting me into action. We quickly draped the blanket over him and rushed him to the M.A.S.H. unit. But the image stayed with me.

I don't know if he survived. The M.A.S.H. units were performing miracles back then, but looking at him, I couldn't imagine how anyone could come back from that. I didn't let myself dwell on it, though. There wasn't time for remorse. More helicopters were landing, more wounded were arriving, and we had to keep moving.

It wasn't just the execution of the mission that hit hard—it was the lives lost to poor planning and arrogance. The base felt heavier and quieter for days afterward as if even the jungle mourned.

That moment haunted me for years without me even realizing it. I buried it deep, just like so much else from Vietnam. It wasn't until decades later, sitting in my psychiatrist Dr. Bornychek's office, that it finally came to the surface.

"Larry," she said, interrupting me as I described that day. "You're holding something back. What aren't you telling me?"

Her question stopped me cold. I didn't want to think about it, let alone say it out loud. But something in her tone, her certainty, pushed me to share.

"There was a man," I began, my voice cracking. "He was on a stretcher... and his legs were gone."

Talking about it felt like peeling off a scab I'd tried to forget was there. But for the first time, the pain didn't feel like mine alone. Dr. Bornychek nodded, listening without judgment. She didn't say much, but her presence was enough.

By bringing it into the light, I started letting go of that moment's hold on me. It didn't erase it, but it lessened the weight.

The war had a way of packing your mind with moments you didn't want to remember and leaving gaps where others should have been. After unloading the wounded that day, I did what I'd done many times before—I pushed the memory into a corner and kept moving. But not all of it stayed buried. The war didn't let you forget for long.

Some memories, though, weren't about trauma—they were about survival, about the strange mix of chaos and routine that became our daily lives. The absurdity of war sometimes surfaced in the quiet moments between the fighting, reminding us that life went on in its own way, even in the darkest times.

***

One afternoon, during a lull in the action, Carl and I practiced our shots. I'd just dropped a round into the mortar tube when, for some reason, I instinctively ducked and covered my ears, which wasn't something we normally did under attack. Carl did the same.

"Did it fire?" he asked, looking at me.

"I don't know. Did you see it?"

"No. I didn't hear it either."

Neither of us knew if the round had gone off. Even in daylight, inside a mortar tube, it was dark, so someone had to check.

"Rock, paper, scissors," Carl suggested.

I lost.

With a flashlight in hand, I cautiously approached the tube. I didn't look directly in, instead angling the light past the opening.

"I don't see it," I said, stepping back.

Carl took his turn. "It's in there," he confirmed.

Now came the real challenge: getting it out. One of us would have to dump the round while the other caught it.

"I'll dump," I volunteered. "You catch."

Slowly, I lifted the tube out of its base and tilted it. The mortar round began to slide. Carl positioned his hand at the bottom to catch it safely. At that exact moment, our officer and the gunnery sergeant arrived.

"Stop!" the officer barked.

I froze, the mortar precariously balanced.

"What do you want me to do?" I asked. "Put it back down?"

He didn't answer, but the gunnery sergeant behind him shook his head and pointed at the officer, silently mouthing, "He's nuts."

"No," I confidently stated, ignoring the command. If I had let the mortar hit the bottom, Carl and I would've both been dead.

I continued tilting the tube. The round slid out, and Carl expertly caught it, securing the firing pin. He walked over and handed it to the officer.

"Here. It's safe now," Carl said.

The officer placed it on a nearby bunker, his face pale.

"Next time, let me know first," he stammered. "I'll evacuate part of the base."

Carl and I exchanged a glance. "That was our fourth one," I said casually.

The officer's eyes widened. He didn't say another word; he just turned and walked away, the gunnery sergeant trailing behind, chuckling to himself.

The lieutenant's behavior didn't exactly surprise us. During all the months I spent on that base, I never saw him check in during an attack—not once. He never came down to the pit to see how we were doing, never gave a word of encouragement, and certainly didn't stick around to get his hands dirty. He was nowhere to be found when the base was under fire, always disappearing to some unseen corner.

The gunnery sergeant wasn't much different. Sure, he'd occasionally show up on base, but he never came to the mortar pit during combat. Clearly, they both preferred the relative safety of their hiding spots, far removed from the danger we faced nightly.

We didn't expect much from them, but their absence during critical moments spoke volumes. It wasn't resentment exactly—it was more like a grim understanding. They weren't going to help us, so we'd learned to rely on ourselves and each other. In a way, it made our bond in the pit stronger, knowing we had no backup coming.

***

As Christmas approached, the attacks continued unabated. The nights blurred together in a cacophony of explosions, sand, and smoke. Carl had ordered aerial rounds—special mortars designed to detonate mid-air and scatter shrapnel over a wide radius—but they never arrived. The missing shipment gnawed at him, though he didn't let it show.

One night, in the middle of an attack, Carl crouched low, his eye glued to the mortar sight. The sand under our feet was relentless, shifting and swallowing the base of the tube with every round fired. Carl constantly adjusted, his left ear inches from the tube's deafening roar. Years later, he'd blame his hearing loss on nights like these.

I was in my usual rhythm, feeding the tube round after round, and the heat of the blasts was constant on my face.

Then, without warning, I found myself flat on the ground in the pit. My head spun as I registered Carl lying nearby, staring at me with wide eyes.

"What the hell just happened?" I managed to croak.

Carl didn't answer. "Get up. I'll explain later," he barked, already back at his post.

The attack ended hours later, the silence ringing louder than the explosions. Carl led me to the back of the pit, where a wooden sign carved with the word "Peacemaker" hung above the sandbags. He pointed at it, and I saw a jagged hole torn clean through the wood. The sandbags beneath it were riddled with shrapnel.

"That aerial round? They got one," Carl said. "It exploded just outside the fence."

He explained how he'd seen the flash through his sight and reacted instinctively, throwing himself to the ground and pulling me with him. The shrapnel had torn through the pit exactly where I'd been standing.

"That would've taken your head clean off," Carl said matter-of-factly.

I didn't know what to say. "Thanks," I muttered. Carl just shrugged. It wasn't heroics for him—it was just what you did for the guy next to you.

***

We had a perimeter around the mortar pit, a necessity we'd built ourselves after realizing how exposed we were. On another chaotic night, Carl stopped mid-shot, his gaze locked on something beyond the pit.

"What is it?" I asked, following his eyes.

"Shadows," he said. "Along the perimeter."

I froze. If the enemy had breached the perimeter, we were sitting ducks. Carl didn't raise his weapon, though. "They'd have killed us by now if they were the enemy."

After the attack ended, we cautiously peered over the sandbags. Four Navy SEALs stood along the perimeter as if watching a performance. They weren't wearing flak jackets—their standard body armor or helmets—just their boonie hats and standard-issue camo.

When they saw us looking, they started clapping. Slow at first, then with more enthusiasm. Carl and I exchanged a look, unsure whether to laugh or yell.

"Well," Carl said finally, "I'm glad they weren't the enemy."

They were totally impressed with how we were defending the base.

They were totally impressed with how we were defending the base. They were out there without any protection because they felt safe, knowing we were doing the job of keeping them and the entire base safe.

The SEALs nodded approvingly and disappeared into the night. Their support meant more than any official commendation could.

***

One day, two SEALs came down to the pit and invited me to visit their barracks—a rare privilege. As we walked together, I couldn't help but feel a mix of pride and unease. That's when we encountered him—the boot lieutenant.

He stood on the step like he was posing for a recruitment poster, his pants perfectly creased, boots polished to a mirror shine, and insignia gleaming on his lapel. Everything about him screamed newbie.

As we passed, he barked, "Sailors! Come back here and salute me!"

I kept walking, with one of the SEALs on each side of me. One of them turned and shot back, "Who the fuck do you think you are?"

The lieutenant persistently chased after us, yelling about protocol and respect. When we reached the SEAL barracks, the SEAL lieutenant met us at the door as the SEALs were laughing.

The SEAL lieutenant shifted his expression from curiosity to irritation. "Why are you laughing?"

"You'll find out. Go to the door!" they snarked, glancing at the approaching newbie.

"Do you know where you are?" he asked the rookie lieutenant.

"I don't care," the lieutenant snapped. "I want them to salute me!"

"You don't have any authorization to be here. You're not coming in, and they're not coming out. And you're certainly not getting a salute," the SEALs' lieutenant said firmly. "So here are your options," he continued with more intensity in his voice. "Leave, now. And don't ever say anything to them again because you don't need a salute from them."

Meanwhile, the newbie lieutenant proceeded to scream at the SEALs' lieutenant.

With an air of calm that was somehow more intimidating than anger, the SEAL lieutenant pulled out his .45, chambered a round, and leveled it at the rookie's head through the screen door.

"You've got three seconds to leave," he said, his voice icy. "Or I'll shoot your ass, and then you'll be dead."

The rookie turned pale, stumbled back, and bolted down the road. The SEALs burst into laughter, slapping each other on the back.

"You're lucky he didn't wet his pants," one of them joked. I wasn't so sure it hadn't happened.

***

Two SEALs appeared at the pit the next day, grinning like they were up to no good.

"Hey, Larry," one said, leaning casually against the sandbags. "Come on up to the barracks with us."

I narrowed my eyes, suspicious. "That doesn't sound like something I want to be doing."

"Oh, c'mon," the other said, his grin widening. "We're gonna have some fun."

Fun, huh? The last time they'd dragged me into something, it had almost gotten me killed—or court-martialed. "All right," I said, sighing.

"But if this gets me in trouble…"

"You'll be fine," the first SEAL said, clapping me on the back.

I followed them to the SEAL barracks, nerves prickling at the back of my neck. The rookie lieutenant from the other day was nowhere to be seen, which eased my tension. When we walked inside, I froze.

The SEALs were sitting around a table, unscrewing grenades like they were tinkering with toys. One held the top of a grenade, carefully removing the firing mechanism, while another reassembled a "dummy" version.

"What the hell are you guys doing?" I asked, my voice a mix of confusion and disbelief.

One of them glanced up and smirked. "Relax, Larry. We're just taking the fire pins out. Turning them into dummies."

I wasn't sure how this was supposed to reassure me. "You know, this doesn't seem like something I want to be involved in."

"Too late," one of them said, laughing. "You're already here."

Meanwhile, their lieutenant had slipped into the barracks where the rookie officer was staying. He didn't say much—just enough to let the others know they might want to clear out. "Go grab a beer," he suggested casually. "Or a sandwich. Just… don't be here."

They didn't ask questions. Soon, the room was empty except for the rookie.

Two SEALs, grenades in hand, took one side of the building. I followed another pair to the opposite side. They moved with precision, a silent language passing between them. One peeked through the screen, spotting the rookie standing inside, oblivious to what was about to happen.

"All right," one whispered. "Here we go."

The doors creaked open just wide enough to toss in the four gre-nades. The spoons flew off as the grenades hit the ground with sharp metallic pings, landing in a perfect circle around the rookie.

"Bing. Bing. Bing. Bing," one of the SEALs muttered, grinning.

From outside, I watched the rookie's face twist in horror as he real-ized what surrounded him. He didn't scream, didn't move—just froze, his eyes darting between the grenades.

The SEAL holding the door leaned down and pressed his weight against it. The rookie finally broke free of his shock and lunged for the exit, slamming into the door only to be thrown back onto the floor.

Outside, we waited for a beat, then let go of the door and walked away, leaving the rookie to figure out the grenades weren't live.

In a place where survival was the only real goal, these moments of madness weren't just pranks—they were a way to stay sane, a remind-er that we were still human.

***

Later, as we strolled back down the road, I could hear the commotion behind us—the rookie finally piecing together what had happened. By the time we reached the pit, I'd already written the guy off as a future problem. But I underestimated him.

From that day on, if the rookie saw me coming, he'd turn tail and walk the other way. He ducked into barracks he didn't belong to, avoided common areas, and acted like I was the plague.

The SEALs, of course, found this hilarious. "He went to the captain," one of them told me a few days later, barely able to contain his laughter. "Said he had to get off the base. Claimed his life was in jeopardy."

"And?" I asked.

"They shipped him out."

"Good riddance," I muttered, shaking my head. "You SEALs get me into more trouble than I can handle."

They just grinned. "Nah, you're one of us now. Trouble comes with the territory."

Nam Can wasn't just a base—it was a blend of mayhem, camaraderie, and absurdity, forging bonds stronger than steel. Every prank, every stolen fridge, every mortar round was part of a shared survival.

The jungle may have surrounded us, but moments like these made us feel alive. And in a war where death was always close, that was everything. But in the back of my mind, I knew—chaos was what we were used to. Stillness, when it came, was its own kind of threat.

Monkey See, Monkey Do

But it is doubtful that Baby ever saw a sailor brace his right foot on the inside of a mortar barrel when he was sighting in. Baby is a five-pound squirrel monkey that has been adopted by U.S. Navymen who man the base defense mortar pits at Nam Can naval base, 180 miles southwest of Saigon. Baby provides plenty of diversion for the sailors' long, often boring days at the remote post deep in the Ca Mau Peninsula, even if she isn't too hep on safety procedures. (Photo by PH1 Harve P. Shiplett)

CHAPTER 6

A Christmas Like No Other

"It's too quiet," Carl said, his voice breaking the stillness.

Carl and I volunteered to stay on duty that Christmas Eve, choosing to hold the line while everyone else took advantage of the ceasefire.

At Nam Can, most holidays passed us by without much notice. Veterans Day and Memorial Day came and went without fanfare. There were no truce agreements, no acknowledgment from the other side that these dates mattered to us.

But Christmas was different. Maybe it was the symbolism, the birth of Christ, or just a universal acknowledgment of its significance. Either way, a ceasefire was called, and the guns fell silent for the first time in months.

It wasn't like there were celebrations or even distractions to enjoy on the base—no bars, no villages to escape to.

The rest of the crew took the opportunity to be off duty, scattered around the base in relative stillness. For us, the stillness was exactly what unnerved us.

By dusk, a strange quiet had settled over Nam Can. Usually, we'd be shooting mortars from dusk to dawn, a relentless rhythm to keep the enemy at bay. That night, we didn't fire a single shot.

Sitting on the edge of the sandbag bunker surrounding the mortar pit, Carl and I barely spoke. There wasn't much to say. The moonless sky hung heavy above us, and the jungle's usual hum seemed distant, muted.

The silence didn't feel peaceful like it should on Christmas Eve—it felt like the kind of quiet that hides something.

I nodded, scanning the horizon. "Way too quiet."

Before we could say anything else, the sound cut through the night—a distant, unmistakable *"Whoop, whoop, whoop!"* firing off three miles in the distance.

"Mortars," Carl said, already on his feet.

Not one mortar, but three. Usually, the enemy fired 10 to 15 rounds, packed up their equipment, and vanished before we could retaliate. But tonight, they'd had all day to prepare. With three mortars firing in unison, they must have brought hundreds of rounds—200, maybe 300. The first bombardment roared toward us; the sound chillingly clear even from three miles away.

"Incoming!" I shouted instinctively, though there was no one around to hear it. It was just the two of us.

The communication bunker was to the left of our pit, where one guy manned the radio. We scrambled toward the communication bunker, dodging through the darkness as the first rounds landed.

The blasts were distant enough to give us time, but close enough to shake the ground beneath our boots. The entrance wasn't directly exposed; it was designed with a protective wall so a grenade or stray round couldn't be easily thrown straight in.

Carl and I dove through the opening, landing on top of each other in the narrow space by the doorway. The comms operator didn't flinch. He shoved a piece of paper into Carl's hand—the coordinates for the incoming fire.

"Coordinates," he said, his voice tight.

Carl and I didn't need the paper to know where the mortars came from. They could only set up two places within range of our base, and the sound told us all we needed to know. We bolted back to the pit, the pounding of our boots drowned by the increasingly chaotic noise of mortar fire.

***

The mortar was covered with a poncho to keep the rain out, and the barrel was capped with a helmet for good measure. Carl yanked the cover off, and I rushed to grab the rounds. We didn't wait to aim; there was no time. As Carl worked to swing the mortar into position, I began firing, the concussive booms echoing across the base.

Their rounds landed all around us, but we had no idea where exactly. Carl and I talked about that a lot—while we were under attack, neither of us looked up or around to see where the rounds were landing. It felt unnecessary. It would take too much time. We weren't dead, so they weren't landing on us. Instead, we focused entirely on the task at hand.

Meanwhile, I was back grabbing rounds. I didn't even bother to check how many powder bags they had on them. I picked them up, muttering, "Whatever, this'll do."

I started throwing them into the tube, one after another.

"We have to make noise," I yelled over the commotion. "Let them know we're firing back!"

Carl nodded, wrenching the mortar around to face the incoming fire. His movements were deliberate, even as I loaded round after round with a force born of desperation. I didn't check the number of powder bags and didn't think about precision—just volume. The faster we fired, the more likely we were to disrupt them.

Minutes blurred into an eternity. My hands moved on instinct, grabbing rounds, loading, firing. Carl leaned into the sight, trying to line up the shots as the mortar's barrel heated.

"Throw them faster!" he shouted.

"I'm going as fast as I can!" I snapped back; my voice strained from the effort.

We kept firing, sending round after round into the night. Maybe two minutes in—though it felt like hours—the other crew members showed up, scrambling to their positions. They handed me rounds, helping me keep momentum while Carl focused on aligning the mortar.

Every second felt like a countdown to disaster.

Their presence was a relief, but the tension in the air was stifling. Every second felt like a countdown to disaster.

Carl kept his eye glued to the sight, his arm resting on the tube as he adjusted the angle. The metal was so hot that I could see the tension in his posture, but he didn't flinch. I grabbed another round, and as I slid it into the tube, the flame brushed right past my hand. It stung, but there was no time to process it. I was already reaching for the next round.

"Look at the tube!" one of the ammo handlers yelled, his voice cutting through the noise.

We took the briefest pause—a fraction of a second that felt like an eternity—and glanced at the tube. The bottom 12 to 16 inches of it were glowing red-hot, the heat from the constant firing turning the steel into something out of a nightmare.

Seeing it made my stomach drop but stopping wasn't an option. We all knew that. We didn't have time to cool it down properly. We didn't have water—just desperation. We resorted to the most absurd solution imaginable.

"Pee on it!" Carl barked.

And so, we did. In the middle of a firefight, with rounds landing dangerously close, we cooled the barrel with our ingenuity and a complete lack of shame.

***

The tube hissed and cooled just enough for us to keep firing. The other mortar crews had finally arrived, adding their firepower to ours, and the air buzzed with the deafening symphony of outgoing and incoming rounds. Navy helicopters had been called in, but the gunships needed time to warm up their jets before they could take off.

"Don't stop shooting," the communication operator relayed. "Keep them pinned until the gunships can take over."

Carl and I redoubled our efforts, directing our fire toward the coordinates we knew so well. The mortars were still hitting dangerously close, and the enemy was relentless in their assault.

Tower One's voice crackled through the comms again. "Second tube! They're on the fence line!"

The words hit like a jolt. The enemy had adjusted, walking their mortars straight along the jagged perimeter. Our fence wasn't a straight line—it zigzagged, reflecting the unpredictable terrain. The precision of their fire told us all we needed to know—someone on the base was feeding them coordinates, guiding their shots with chilling accuracy.

Our new target meant swinging the mortar's angle dramatically, which was problematic. Three towering communication masts stood between us and the fence line, their stabilizing wires crisscrossing like invisible tripwires.

There were no lights on the towers—they were meant to be hidden in the darkness, a deliberate effort to avoid turning them into beacons for enemy fire. But for us, they were obstacles, and we had no margin for error.

Carl swung the mortar, aligning it toward the new threat. The stakes we used for quick adjustments were useless for this angle, and the elevation needed to clear the nearby communication towers was precariously tight.

Carl and I stared at the mortar, its barrel aimed directly between the dark outlines of the communication towers. The wires supporting the towers loomed like invisible traps in the night. There was no room for error—not even a fraction.

"What's the range?" I asked, my voice tense.

"Four bags!" he shouted back, my hands already reaching for a round. Four bags meant about a mile, just enough to clear the fence line and hopefully avoid the towers.

Carl hesitated, his eyes darting between the mortar's angle and the faint shadows of the towers ahead.

"One round," he said, his tone absolute. "Just one!"

I froze, my hands clutching the round. "One round? Are you serious?" My voice cracked with disbelief. This wasn't the time for half-measures.

"One round!" he yelled again, his authority cutting through my resistance.

The seconds stretched unbearably long as Carl bent low, his face inches from the tube as he sighted it by eye. It was sheer luck, a mix of experience, and desperation. He straightened, locking eyes with me. "Do it."

I dropped the round into the tube and ducked, my heart pounding as it fired. The mortar's recoil vibrated through the pit, and we both braced for impact.

Seconds later, Tower One's voice broke through the comms: "Secondary! Secondary!" The tower reported an explosion—they'd seen the explosion in the air—and we had missed the tower!

Carl and I exchanged glances, barely daring to breathe. We fired again, the tension easing slightly with each successive round. The mortars on the fence line had been neutralized, the catastrophic blast silencing their fire. Whatever we hit had been enough to stop them.

The last round they'd managed to fire landed just outside our pit, close enough to catch my breath. One more adjustment, one more second of their spotter calling out coordinates, and that round would've landed among us. But they didn't get that chance.

We were just one shot away from death, one shot away from our base taking a hit that would've changed everything.

***

With the fence line secured, the chaos gradually began to subside. The gunships finally roared overhead, their presence a reassurance that the night's worst was behind us.

Carl leaned against the edge of the pit, wiping his forehead with the back of his hand. "We blew them up with one damn round," he muttered, a mix of exhaustion and pride in his voice.

I nodded, my ears ringing from the barrage. "Whatever it was, it worked."

The night wasn't over, but the immediate threat had passed.

We stayed there for a moment, letting the adrenaline ebb as the acrid smell of gunpowder lingered in the air. The night wasn't over, but the immediate threat had passed. The jungle was alive again with distant sounds, the echoes of battle fading into the background.

"Hell of a Christmas," Carl said, a faint grin breaking through his weariness.

I chuckled despite myself. "Yeah. One for the books."

The gunships carried on their patrol, their blades slicing through the night as we sat in the sandbagged pit.

We didn't have the luxury of celebrating. The night wasn't over, and neither was the war. But for a brief moment, as the helicopters roared overhead, we let ourselves feel something close to triumph.

***

The jungle was damp from the aftermath of the previous night's attack when the Navy SEALs showed up at our pit the next morning. They wasted no time, their presence commanding as ever.

"Grab your gear," one of them said, his voice low and firm. "We're heading out to the road."

Carl and I exchanged a glance but didn't question it. When the SEALs said, "Let's go," you went. We climbed onto a PBR and sped down the murky river. The boat sliced through the water, its engine a low rumble against the natural symphony of the jungle. It wasn't a long ride, but the tension made it feel like an eternity.

When the PBR came to a stop, we got off and followed the SEALs into the dense jungle. The trail was narrow, overgrown, and stifling, with humid air clinging to our skin. After a short trek, the jungle opened up to reveal what remained of the road—a wide, flat expanse littered with debris.

The scene before us was nothing short of devastation. Pieces of mortar rounds and shattered equipment were scattered everywhere, jagged remnants of the enemy's weapons. The ground was pocked with craters, some shallow, others deep enough to swallow a man. One hole in particular stood out—a massive cavity where something had clearly exploded with catastrophic force.

But there were no bodies.

Carl knelt down, inspecting a shard of metal. "No blood, no body parts," he muttered.

The SEAL closest to us nodded. "They cleaned up before we got here. Whatever was left, they took it with them."

I stepped forward, my boots crunching against broken fragments of mortar tubes and other indistinguishable wreckage. The destruction was undeniable, not just from one or two well-placed rounds. It was systematic and thorough—a testament to our relentless fire.

The SEALs conferred briefly before giving us the tally: six confirmed kills. They estimated that the team had likely been made up of four to eight men. While not all had been killed, the scale of destruction left little room for doubt—we'd done significant damage.

"Six of theirs, at least," one of the SEALs said. His tone wasn't celebratory, just matter of fact.

I glanced at Carl, who was scanning the area with his usual intensity. The absence of bodies didn't sit right with me, but the evidence told its own story. Whatever we'd hit in that cataclysmic blast had obliterated more than just equipment.

The road itself was covered in marks from our mortars. Holes left in the ground, their edges blackened and raw. One huge hole marked the explosion's epicenter that had turned the tide of the fight. It wasn't just a hit—it was a statement.

For days afterward, the jungle seemed quieter. The sporadic mortar fire that had become our grim routine wasn't gone entirely, but it was no longer relentless. They shot at us less frequently—every two or three days instead of every night.

Carl and I speculated about the change. "Maybe we hit them harder than we thought," he said one evening as we loaded up rounds for another night. "Took out some of their best."

It wasn't just a matter of numbers; it felt deeper than that. Losing six men—possibly friends, brothers, or fathers—had shaken them. It wasn't the kind of loss that drove you to fight harder; it was the kind that made you question whether the fight was worth it at all.

Whatever the reason, their pride and morale had taken a hit, and for now, it seemed to work in our favor. The tension eased ever so slightly, but we knew better than to let our guard down. Quiet in the jungle didn't mean peace—it meant something was coming.

Still, as we left the remains of the road that day and climbed back onto the PBR, there was a sense of grim satisfaction. Not triumph, exactly, but a hardened understanding of what we'd accomplished. Six fewer mortars to haunt our nights, six fewer rounds aimed at our base.

The river carried us back toward Nam Can, the jungle swallowing the road behind us. We didn't speak much on the ride back; each of us lost in our own thoughts. The night's mayhem had subsided, but calm was always temporary in Vietnam. We'd live to see another fight, which was enough for now.

***

The orders came quietly, as they always did, marking the end of my year in-country. My time at Nam Can was up, and the Navy was sending me home. Most guys would have felt relief at the prospect, but I wasn't ready to leave. Not yet.

Before my departure, I'd even tried to extend my stay. The SEALs at Nam Can needed a new mechanic for their river patrol boats, and I saw it as a chance to stay useful. The role was far more dangerous than firing mortars every night, but I figured I could handle it if I'd survived this long.

The Navy disagreed.

"You've got to be crazy to want that job," someone higher up had said, rejecting my application outright. That was that. With orders in hand, I said my goodbyes, boarded a helicopter, and flew to Saigon to begin the checkout process.

***

Saigon had its own rhythms, nothing like the jungle or the relentless chaos of Nam Can. It was surreal to find myself in the city, knowing that just days ago, I'd been dodging mortar fire. But the transition wasn't as smooth as stepping off a helicopter and boarding a plane home.

Before anyone could leave Vietnam, we had to go through a week-long process to ensure we were clean—literally. Too many GIs had become hooked on heroin during their time in-country, and the military had finally realized the mistake of sending addicts home without addressing the problem. So, we were subjected to blood and urine tests and held in limbo until we got the all-clear.

I passed, but the waiting didn't end there. My orders still hadn't caught up to me, leaving me stuck in Saigon with no clear timeline for departure. I needed a place to stay, so I returned to the barracks where I'd first arrived in Vietnam. It was a convenient place to stay—being both free and where I'd eventually collect my orders.

The familiarity of the barracks was both a comfort and a sharp reminder of how much had changed since my first day. Back then, I was a rookie, standing on a rooftop guard without any ammunition, entirely unprepared for what was ahead.

It only took 12 months to turn this hockey player into a battle-hardened Navy sailor, my M16 slung across my chest—for ease of use, as the SEALs taught me. It was faster to access than in a sling like I was initially taught. It was loaded with sixty rounds at all times and set to fully automatic—I didn't even know what semi-automatic was.

***

The man behind the desk at the barracks office clearly hadn't spent a day in the jungle. He wore a standard green shirt, no camouflage, clean and unmarked without any signal of his rank, and spoke with an air of detachment that grated on me. When I approached the small drive-through-style window to check in, I could already tell this wouldn't go well.

"I'll need you to surrender your weapon," he said, reaching through the window toward me.

I stared at him in disbelief. "Not happening."

His hand froze mid-reach, and I took a deliberate step back, my grip tightening on the M16 slung across my chest. I let a round into the chamber and pointed at his chest. "This is still a war zone," I said evenly. "You're not taking my gun."

Before he could respond, I brought the barrel level with his chest. His eyes widened, and the room behind him went deathly silent. I glanced past him to see the other staff ducking under their desks, clearly convinced I was about to kill this guy, and they didn't want to be next.

"You're not taking my weapon," I repeated, my voice steady.

For a moment, the only sound was the tension in the air, thick enough to choke on. Then, with one final glance at the man's frozen expression, I backed away, being sure not to turn my back, keeping my weapon aimed at the window until I was out the door.

Out on the street, I flagged down a bicycle taxi—a contraption with a seat in front for passengers. I climbed in, my weapon still slung across my chest, and instructed the driver to take me to the Saigon Hilton.

The hotel was a stark contrast to the barracks. A three-star oasis with a rooftop pool, garden, and bar, it was as far removed from the war as possible while still in Vietnam. From the roof, I could see the city sprawling below me and, in the distance, the flashes of gunfire and explosions on the perimeter of Saigon. It was a surreal juxtaposition, a moment of calm while the war raged on just beyond the city limits.

I stayed at the Hilton for two days, enjoying the rare comfort of a proper bed and hot meals. On the second evening, as I sat at the bar nursing a drink, I spotted a familiar face—Reichel, one of the guys from the mortar team.

"Bob!" I called, standing to greet him. "What are you doing here?"

"Got my orders," he said with a grin. "Heading home."

"Guess we're in the same boat," I replied, patting him on the shoulder. "You can crash in my room if you want. I've got two queen beds on the fourth floor and a balcony looking out over the city. No sense paying for another."

Reichel accepted, and for the next two days, we shared the room, catching up and laughing at memories that already felt like they belonged to another lifetime.

Eventually, I had to face the barracks again. Reichel listened as I told him what had happened with the man at the window. He chuckled. "Well, guess we'll find out what they're going to do to ya—we'll see if they're waiting to lock you up."

When I returned, the man from before was gone, replaced entirely by someone else. I still had my weapon slung across my chest as I approached the window, but this time, there was no confrontation.

"Your orders will be here tomorrow," the new clerk said.

I nodded, backing away from the window just as cautiously as before. Then I turned and left, relieved there were no raised voices or tense standoffs this time.

After reuniting with Reichel, he mentioned that they told him his orders would be ready in about a week.

The next day, my orders came through. I was to report to the USS *Fulton*, which was in dry dock in North Carolina. But before that, I had two weeks of leave, two weeks to step away from the war and try to remember what life was like outside of Vietnam.

When I finally boarded the plane at the Air Force Base, I handed over my M16 to a Marine standing guard. He pointed to a massive pile of rifles stacked four feet tall near the door. It was a strange sight—a mountain of weapons discarded as soldiers crossed the threshold from war to home.

I exhaled deeply as I stepped onto the plane and found my seat. The weight of the last year was slowly beginning to lift. I was heading home for the first time in what felt like forever.

The plane's engines hummed softly as we taxied down the runway, the lights of Saigon fading into the distance. The weight of my M16 was gone, surrendered to the towering pile of rifles at the base, a symbol of the year I was leaving behind. But even as I sat in that cramped seat, staring out at the inky black sky, I couldn't shake the sense that a part of me was still tethered to Vietnam.

The flight out was long, with refueling stops in Singapore and Alaska before finally landing in California. Each leg of the journey felt surreal, like I was moving through a dream where the rules of reality had been suspended.

When we touched down at a military airfield in California, I was handed some travel pay—enough to find a motel room and catch my final flight home. It all was almost laughable. After everything I'd been through, I was here navigating logistics like any other traveler.

I checked into a small motel, and my sea bag was almost empty. My civilian clothes, unused and forgotten in the jungle, had succumbed to mold and rot. All I had left were the jungle greens I was wearing, their faded camouflage a stark reminder of the world I'd just left behind.

The next day, I walked through the airport, my camouflage standing out among the civilian crowd. Most people avoided eye contact, and their glances quickly redirected away from me. When I stepped off the plane, I had no idea how people felt about this war that I'd been drafted into. We didn't know about the protests, so the anger surprised me. Without access to T.V. and only military-run radio, that type of news wasn't shared.

One man stepped into my path.

"Baby killer," he exclaimed, his voice low and harsh.

He took a step forward, spitting directly at me.

He was a fool to get that close.

I didn't think. I didn't need to. My fist shot forward, quick and sharp, honed by the lessons the SEALs had taught me. No wind-up, no hesitation—just a clean strike. His teeth cracked under the impact, and he crumpled to the floor.

I walked away without a word, my heart pounding but my steps steady. The crowd around me didn't interfere. Their silence spoke volumes. By the time I reached my gate, the moment already felt like a distant memory.

***

The flight to Wisconsin was quieter, and the transition back to civilian life slowly crept in. When I landed, my girlfriend was waiting. We went straight to a store, and I bought civilian clothes. The fabric felt strange, almost foreign, as I traded my camouflage for something softer, less burdened by the weight of memory.

Eventually, I returned to New Jersey, to the familiarity of home and family. But the transition wasn't seamless. I could still hear the mortar rounds, feel the humid weight of the jungle air, and see the faces of the men I'd fought alongside. It seemed I hadn't really left after all.

***

Looking back, my year in Vietnam taught me more than I could ever have imagined. It taught me resilience—the kind that comes from firing mortars into the night with a red-hot tube and no guarantees of survival. It taught me loyalty, forged in the uncertainty of battle alongside men who would risk their lives for each other without hesitation. And it taught me the cost of war—not just in lives lost but in the scars it leaves behind, both visible and unseen.

As I prepared to meet my next assignment on the USS *Fulton*, I couldn't help but carry these lessons. They were a part of me now, as much as the memories of the jungle and the camaraderie of the pit. And though the war was behind me, its echoes would remain, shaping the man I was becoming.

For now, though, I had these two weeks at home. That was more than enough. Home wasn't permanent, and I knew it. I wasn't done with my four-year draft just yet—the Navy still had plans for me, and as I prepared to report to my next assignment, I wondered what challenges awaited me beyond the jungles of Vietnam.

CHAPTER 7

ORDERS AND OUTRAGE

"What's my assignment on the USS Fulton?" I asked at personnel, fully expecting something to match the intensity of what I'd just left behind.

When I heard the response, I blinked. "You've got to be kidding me."

The quiet rhythm of my civilian days didn't last long. After my leave in New Jersey, I made my way to North Carolina to report to the USS *Fulton*. The *Fulton* was a sub tender—a ship designed to service submarines—and wasn't even ready to leave port when I arrived. It sat in dry dock, an artifact of an earlier era.

The *Fulton's* keel was laid around 1940, and by the time I boarded it in 1972, it showed its age. It had survived World War II and earned its share of battle stars when it serviced diesel subs. Decades later, the Navy was patching it up to keep it afloat a little longer.

They didn't know what to do with me when I first stepped aboard. The ship wasn't fully operational yet, and no immediate assignment was waiting for me. "Hang around," someone said, waving me off like an afterthought. I took that as permission to explore the town, trying to readjust to life in the States.

It wasn't easy. I was still on edge, constantly scanning my surroundings for threats that weren't there. Dodging bullets had become second nature, and the absence of my M16 left me feeling exposed. My mind churned with the questions that had kept me alive in Vietnam: *Where's the danger? Who's got the gun? Why don't I have mine?*

I was only 19—still a teenager—but I felt decades older, the war having etched itself into every corner of my psyche.

***

When the *Fulton* finally prepared to leave dry dock, the news of my assignment nearly knocked me off my feet.

"Mess hall duty," the clerk said flatly.

I laughed in disbelief. "Mess cooking? You've got to be kidding me. I'm a combat veteran. I just walked out of Vietnam and you're telling me to cook?"

The man behind the counter shrugged. "Orders are orders."

Refusing to take this lying down, I left personnel and headed straight to the mess hall office. The man in charge—a middle-aged sailor in a white uniform—sat behind a desk, shuffling papers with an air of boredom. I held my orders tightly in my hand, refusing to let him take control of my next move.

"I'm here about the mess hall assignment," I said, keeping my voice calm.

He looked up briefly. "Report to the mess cooks' bunk area."

I didn't budge. "No," I said flatly. "I'm not going to mess cooking. If

I do, someone's going to get hurt—or somebody's going to die—and it's not going to be me."

His jaw dropped. He stared at me, frozen, his face a mix of shock and disbelief. I didn't give him time to respond. Holding my orders firmly, I stood and walked out, heading directly across the hall to the chaplain's office.

***

I walked a beeline for it, knocked on the door, and heard the chaplain call out, "Come in."

I stepped inside, still dressed in my Navy uniform. I think it was my blues—it might've been my whites—but either way, it was my formal dress. I had my hat on, but as soon as I saw the chaplain wasn't wearing his, I knew saluting wasn't required. That's military protocol: no hat, no salute.

He sat at his desk, looking up from some papers. I walked over and sat down across from him. His calm demeanor contrasted with the turmoil brewing inside me.

"How can I help you, sailor?" he asked, his voice steady.

I sat down, my hands still gripping my orders. "I don't know if you can," I admitted. "But I've got a situation."

He nodded, waiting for me to continue.

"I just walked out of the mess hall office," I began. "They tried to send me to mess cooking. I told the guy in charge that if I went, someone was going to get hurt—or worse—and it wouldn't be me."

The chaplain's eyebrows shot up, but he kept his composure. "And what did he say?"

"Nothing. He just sat there, stunned."

The chaplain held out his hand. "Let me see your orders."

Reluctantly, I handed them over. He skimmed the file, his expression growing more serious with each page. He stood and left the room, saying, "I'll be back." I was left alone to wonder what was coming next.

I sat there, elbows on my knees, staring at the floor. My mind raced with worst-case scenarios.

Was he calling the shore patrol? Was I about to get locked up in the brig? Had I finally pushed my luck too far?

After 45 minutes of sitting with my racing thoughts, I was convinced I would be locked up. My fate was about to be determined by who walked through the door next.

When the chaplain returned, he wasn't alone. Following behind him was another officer—a high-ranking commander with shoulders full of stripes and shoes polished so brightly I could see my reflection in them.

With each stripe representing four years of service, I realized this man had been in the Navy longer than I had been alive. His presence was commanding, and I felt the weight of his experience before he even said a word. His polished shoes, crisp uniform, and the golden oak leaf decorations, which we called scrambled eggs, adorning his cap screamed authority, but there was something else—an air of calm that contrasted sharply with the tension I felt.

The chaplain returned to his seat while the commander stood before me. I instinctively started to rise, but the commander placed a firm hand on my shoulder.

"Stay seated, sailor," he said. His voice was calm, almost reassuring.

I hesitated, torn between protocol and his tone's strange sense of reassurance. I was convinced his job was to keep me calm before the cops came to arrest me.

As I settled back into my chair, he moved to stand beside the chaplain's desk. I really didn't feel comfortable ignoring such a high-ranking officer, so I started to stand up again to salute him.

He did it again. He put his hand on my shoulder and firmly said, "Sailor, just stay seated. You're fine."

The chaplain offered a slight nod of encouragement, his eyes steady on mine. He mouthed in barely a whisper, "It's okay."

The officer's words and the chaplain's reassurance started to help me relax. I began to believe that the outcome wasn't going to result in me being locked up for what I'd done.

The commander's gaze met mine, and he spoke in a measured tone. "You're not going mess cooking," he said. "From this moment forward, you're assigned to my division. Engineering."

I found out this officer was in charge of all engineering aboard the USS *Fulton*. He oversaw everything from the ship's engine room to the various shops that serviced the submarines we supported. He wasn't just a cog in the machine—he ran the entire operation, the backbone of the ship's functionality.

His word carried weight, and at that moment, it carried me out of the mess hall and into a role that finally felt like a step forward instead of a step down.

Relief washed over me so quickly that I almost felt dizzy. "Thank you, sir," I said, my voice barely above a whisper.

The commander nodded. "You'll be assigned to 38 Shop. Report there immediately. They've already been notified. We'll be in touch. I'm sure I'm going to see you again."

With that, he turned and left the room, leaving me alone with the chaplain.

The commander wasn't just making an offhand decision—he'd done his homework. Later, I learned he had taken the time to review my records before making this call. As he'd put it, "There ain't no freaking way I'm sending this combat veteran to mess cooking. The guy just walked out of a jungle, fighting for our country in Vietnam, and you're gonna send him to do a job reserved for boot camp recruits? Not on my watch."

"You'll be fine," the chaplain said, smiling for the first time. "Go on. 38 Shop is waiting for you. Their bunking is on the third deck."

***

When I arrived at 38 Shop, I was greeted by a chief and a first-class officer. The chief was surprisingly laid-back, greeting me casually, "Hey, Burke, what's happening?"

It caught me off guard. It was way more down-to-earth than I was expecting from a chief. "Uh… nothing much, Chief," I stammered.

"Welcome to 38 Shop," he said. "We've decided you're going to be our new supply petty officer."

I glanced down at my sleeve, noting my rank. "Chief, I'm not even a petty officer," I pointed out.

"Don't worry," he said with a grin. "We'll take care of that."

And just like that, I was part of 38 Shop, stepping into a role I'd never trained for. But that was nothing new. I'd never trained to shoot mortars, either, and I'd figured that out just fine. This was one more challenge to tackle—one more way to move forward from the jungle to whatever came next.

As I settled into the role, I learned something that made my head spin. The two guys currently handling the job were both leaving—and I was expected to take over for them. What had been a two-man operation would now be handled by me, alone. I'd have to juggle all the responsibilities they'd been sharing.

Well, this is going to be interesting.

***

The job at 38 Shop was a far cry from the jungle, but it was no cakewalk. Every order I processed required precision—there were no computers, just handwritten chits where I carefully filled out part numbers, descriptions, and submarine designations. A single mistake could derail the whole process.

Once the chits were complete, I took them around the ship for signatures, ending with the commander who'd pulled me out of mess duty. I handled 25 to 30 orders on a typical day, covering everything from writing to delivery. It had been a two-man job before, but now it was just me.

The work was demanding, but I took pride in it. After months of chaos in the jungle, contributing to something critical without dodging mortar fire felt like a different kind of victory.

***

The job had its challenges, but it was rewarding. I wasn't just filling orders—I was helping keep submarines running. The work was demanding, but it gave me a sense of purpose.

The commander noticed my dedication, and over time, our relationship shifted from formal to something closer to friendship. One day, as I brought in a stack of chits, he motioned for me to sit down and close the door.

"I want to tell you something," he said, leaning back in his chair. "You're doing a damn good job."

"Thank you, sir," I replied, caught off guard by the compliment.

He nodded, his expression softening. "And another thing—when it's just you and me in this office, you can drop the 'sir.' Call me by my name."

The offer stunned me. Officers didn't typically invite enlisted men to address them on a first-name basis. It wasn't just about formality—it was about the rigid hierarchy that defined military life. But here was this commander, the man in charge of the entire engineering division, telling me we were on equal footing in private.

"Yes, sir—uh, okay," I said awkwardly, earning a chuckle from him.

From that day on, our dynamic shifted. When the door was closed, we were two people working toward the same goal. This camaraderie was a level I hadn't expected, making the long days at 38 Shop more bearable.

***

Not everyone was as supportive as the commander, though. The officer technically in charge of 38 Shop—a newly minted ensign—had a chip on his shoulder the size of a submarine. He was a former master chief promoted into officer ranks, and he seemed to have it out for me for some reason.

One day, as I was walking past his office, he barked at me to come inside. His tone was harsh, commanding, and entirely unwarranted.

I stepped into his office as he launched into a tirade about nothing in particular. I let him rant as he went on for several minutes, my expression blank.

When he finally paused, I asked flatly, "Are you done?"

He stared at me, momentarily stunned by my lack of respect in response to his tantrum. Without waiting for an answer, I turned and walked out, heading straight for the commander's office to get my next signature.

I said, "I need to talk to you about something." When I explained what had happened, the commander's expression darkened.

"That's unnecessary," he said, his voice firm. "I'll take care of it."

As I left the commander's office, I spotted the officer who had just been yelling at me coming down the hallway. Without breaking stride, I gave him a half-hearted, fake salute—just enough to make my point—and walked right past him without a word.

True to his word, the commander took care of it. The next day, I heard from one of the commander's staff that the ensign had been summoned for a private meeting. Rumor had it the commander was screaming during this private meeting and had threatened to court-martial him if he didn't back off. Whatever was said in that meeting, it worked. The ensign's attitude toward me changed almost overnight.

The ensign said to me in a jovial manner, "I think we got off on the wrong foot. I think what we need to do is start over."

It was just another reminder of how far I'd come. From the turmoil of Vietnam to the structured environment of the *Fulton*, I'd learned to navigate challenges with a mix of grit, humor, and the occasional audacious stunt. And while I didn't always play by the rules, I'd earned the respect of those who mattered. That, more than anything, made my time worthwhile.

***

One day, while going through the endless numbers and codes on the chits, I had an idea. Call it curiosity or boredom, but I decided to see if I could push the system's limits. If the Navy could deliver parts for submarines with such precision, why not something a little more… unconventional?

I decided to try ordering a tank.

Finding the number wasn't easy. Submarines were the Navy's priority, not tanks, so I had to dig through a different set of records. Eventually, I found it—a lengthy sequence of letters and numbers corresponding to an actual tank. I wrote it up like any other order, disguising it as a piece of machinery. The chit looked perfectly legitimate.

As I walked it through the chain of signatures, I couldn't help but wonder if anyone would notice. Most officers simply glanced at the chits before signing off, trusting I knew what I was doing. By the time I reached the commander's office, I was just one signature away from success.

The commander was sharp, though—he'd seen thousands of chits pass across his desk. As he reviewed my work, he paused, his pen hovering over the page.

"I don't recognize this sequence of numbers," he said, his brow furrowing.

I scrambled for an explanation. "Oh, must've been a mistake," I said quickly. "I'll fix it."

He handed the chit back without signing it, and I left his office with a mix of relief and disappointment. I'd come so close to having a tank delivered to the pier, but I knew it was probably for the best that the plan hadn't worked. Seeing a tank being unloaded would've raised far too many questions.

***

The job at 38 Shop was far more critical than I initially realized. It wasn't just about filing orders; I was responsible for procuring the vital components that kept our attack submarines operational. These subs, designed for six-month underwater deployments, relied on everything from air circulation systems to complex reactor cooling components—parts that, if they failed, could end a mission or worse.

As an E-2, I was technically at the bottom of the Navy's hierarchy. Yet somehow, I'd been placed in charge of coordinating these critical systems. My orders spanned motors, electronics, and even reactor systems, with each part requiring detailed, handwritten chits. There were no computers, and every chit had to include precise codes, descriptions, and submarine designations. A single mistake could have far-reaching consequences.

I filled out dozens of these forms daily, ensuring various officers signed them off before reaching the commander. He reviewed every single one, a task he took seriously.

One morning, my chief approached me with the news. "We've got a problem."

One of the submarines had a major issue. It was docked alongside the ship, unable to deploy because of a leaking ball valve in its nuclear reactor's cooling system. The valve controlled radioactive water—both scalding hot and dangerously radioactive. Its failure wasn't just inconvenient; it was catastrophic.

"They've already tried replacing it," the chief explained. "But the new valve is defective too. They can't go out to sea like this."

I was tasked with finding a replacement. This wasn't some off-the-shelf part—it was a titanium valve with specialized seals designed to withstand the reactor's extreme conditions. The commander had already identified the manufacturer in Massachusetts but left the call to me. Whether it was out of trust or practicality, I'm still not sure.

After navigating through all the phone gatekeepers and a string of less-than-helpful staff, I reached the company president on the phone.

"The Navy isn't in the business of waiting," I told him, bluffing a level of authority I didn't have. "We need that valve, and we need it now."

He was hesitant, saying that their only valve in stock was already being processed to go to another ship.

I bluffed a bit more by replying, "No. You'll send that part to our ship immediately."

The company president pushed back a bit more, and I cut him off by asking, "Do you want more Navy contracts?"

To my surprise, after a bit more bluffing on my part, he agreed. The valve was packed and escorted by police directly from Massachusetts to our pier in Connecticut. Meanwhile, the submarine crew prepared the reactor system for installation, using liquid nitrogen to freeze the surrounding pipes.

It was a delicate operation—one mistake could crack the hull or worse.

I ended up helping carry the liquid nitrogen onto the sub. The stuff was so cold it could shatter steel on contact—365 degrees Fahrenheit below 0. We worked in a relay, passing the containers down the submarine's narrow ladders. Once the valve was replaced, the submarine was ready to deploy—only two days behind schedule.

The commander was pleased and made sure I knew it. "You did a great job," he said, handing me another stack of chits—the kind of acknowledgment that made the long hours and high stakes worth it.

***

But the commander's words weren't the only acknowledgment I received. Then came the day I walked into personnel and was greeted with unexpected news: "Burke, you're getting a medal."

At first, I brushed it off. It wasn't until weeks later, as the ceremony approached, that the significance sank in. The medal was for actions during the Christmas attack in Vietnam. The lieutenant had followed through on his promise, submitting me and Carl for recognition.

The ceremony itself was a blur. The ship's captain presided, handing out a few medals before an empty chair next to him raised questions. Then the bells sounded—each one marking the rank of the high-ranking officer stepping aboard. The more bells, the higher the rank.

Moments later, an admiral entered the room. When the admiral approached, I wasn't sure what to do. Do I salute him immediately? Wait until he stops?

My nerves were on edge as he walked over, holding a book and the medal. He read aloud the recognition from the book, citing "above and beyond the call of duty" and "silencing the enemy." It was a Navy and Marine Corps Achievement Medal with a "V" for valor—a distinction I hadn't expected.

The admiral saluted me first, a gesture that caught me off guard, and then pinned the medal onto my uniform.

The admiral saluted me again, and the ceremony was over just like that. As he spun on his heel and left the mess hall, the captain called out, "At ease," signaling everyone to relax.

My friends gathered near the door were already making their opinions known, teasing me with exaggerated gestures.

"Brown-noser, huh, Burke?" one of them muttered with a smirk.

I shook my head, half-smiling. I hadn't asked for any of this, but their jokes were all in good fun. The weight of the medal on my chest was a quiet reminder of that chaotic Christmas night. I didn't dwell on it much, but for a fleeting moment, I let myself feel the honor of it.

I left the ceremony with mixed feelings. In my eyes, I hadn't done anything extraordinary—I'd just done my job. But seeing the respect in the commander's eyes and feeling the medal's weight on my chest, I realized that sometimes, just doing your job can mean everything.

***

Not long after, life aboard the *Fulton* fell into its usual rhythm until news broke that the ship would be deploying to the Mediterranean. When I got the orders, my heart sank.

Italy? After a year in Vietnam and all the adjustments to civilian life I'd struggled with, the thought of heading overseas again was more than I could stomach. I pushed back, even speaking to my commander about it.

"Sir, I just got back. I need to stay in the States."

He shook his head, his tone sympathetic but firm. "Burke, I wish I could, but we need you. No one else can step into your role—not with the time frame we're working under. These subs need to be fully supplied before we leave, and you're the one who knows how to make that happen."

I didn't have a choice. In the weeks leading up to our departure, I worked nonstop, filling orders, double-checking inventories, and ensuring every essential part was onboard. Once we left, there'd be no way to resupply easily. A submarine's maintenance isn't something you can leave to chance. I poured myself into the work, knowing that missing something could jeopardize an entire mission.

Eventually, we set sail for our destination—Sardinia, an island off the coast of Italy. The Mediterranean was beautiful, with rolling blue waves and a coastline that looked like something out of a postcard. But the trip there was anything but serene.

The *Fulton*, slow at the best of times, plodded along at a mere 15 knots, making it feel like we'd never get there. And then we hit a storm.

We saw it coming—a mass of dark clouds on the horizon, churning the ocean into an unpredictable force. The captain tried steering south to avoid it, but time wasn't on our side. Eventually, we had no choice but to push through.

The waves towered over us, some reaching 40 feet high. The ship groaned and tilted, water crashing over the bow. All external decks were locked down, but my buddy Louie and I decided to test our luck.

"We're going out," I told him, grinning despite the danger.

"Why not?" he replied.

We stepped onto the main deck, gripping the railings as the waves heaved the ship back and forth. At one point, the water receded so far from the hull that we could lean over and nearly see the bottom of the ship. Then it came rushing back, a towering wall of water hurtling toward us.

The force of the impact tilted the *Fulton*—nearly 45 degrees—and it felt like we were about to roll completely onto our side. Another wave from the opposite direction slammed us upright, leveling the ship just in time. Surviving what I had in Vietnam left me fearless. What could this ocean do to me that war in Vietnam hadn't already attempted?

***

The Mediterranean greeted us with calm waters and clear skies when the storm passed. The captain declared a swim call, and we eagerly dove into the pristine blue sea. It felt like paradise for a moment—until I noticed the armed guys in boats circling us, ready to fend off any approaching sharks.

Then, the intercom crackled with a cheerful announcement: "Closest land? Two miles straight down." That was all I needed to hear. I climbed out of the water without a second thought—no way was I taking chances with what might be lurking below.

Once we reached Sardinia, life slowed down. My work was done for the time being, and I had the rare luxury of free time. The island was breathtaking, with quaint villages, rolling hills, and the kind of serene beauty I'd only seen in movies. I spent my days exploring, soaking in the local culture, and occasionally indulging in the laid-back Italian lifestyle.

One of my favorite memories from Sardinia involved a tiny Italian restaurant that we stumbled upon. The English-speaking owner had never made a pizza—so we taught him.

Using his brick oven, fresh mozzarella, and a simple sauce, he crafted what might've been the best pizza I'd ever tasted. By the time we left, he'd become the island's unofficial "pizza king."

We also played soccer against the local Italian military. They were skilled, effortlessly maneuvering the ball around us, but in the end, they split up the teams to give us a fighting chance. Even then, it wasn't much of a contest. But the camaraderie made it worth it.

***

One afternoon, while we were hanging out in a small park near the main town square, something unusual caught our attention. Right across the street was a fancy-looking restaurant with outdoor seating—tablecloths, polished silverware, the whole nine yards. It looked like a place for the wealthy, not for guys like us.

We sat in the park, watching the scene play out like something out of a mob movie.

As we sat there, two black cars pulled up and parked out front. From the first car, a group of men stepped out, each one scanning the area like they were on high alert. Their hands rested on their chests, under their coats, in a way that made it clear they were packing heat. A couple of them moved toward the restaurant door while the others stayed behind, watching the street like hawks.

Moments later, a man got out of the second car. He was dressed sharp, and you could tell right away he wasn't just anyone. A few more men followed him, sticking close like shadows. They walked him straight to the restaurant, their eyes darting around, ready for trouble.

Inside, the commotion began. Customers who had been eating their meals suddenly started pouring out of the place, looking like they couldn't leave fast enough. Chairs scraped, waiters froze mid-step, and the restaurant emptied out in minutes.

We sat in the park, watching the scene play out like something out of a mob movie. Turns out, the man who'd just arrived was a high-ranking mafia figure who wasn't there to mix with the locals. He wanted the restaurant all to himself, and his men made sure it happened.

From that moment on, the place stayed quiet—no customers, no chatter, just the sound of the wind blowing through the street. We didn't stick around after that. It was a reminder that power moved in ways we didn't fully understand, even in a place as beautiful as Sardinia.

***

Toward the end of our 6-month deployment, we encountered the Sardinian version of bumper cars. Louie and I, along with a few other sailors, couldn't resist showing the locals how it was done.

At first, they drove timidly in circles, but they got the idea when we started ramming into each other with force. By the time we left, the line for the ride had doubled, and the operator thanked us for teaching his customers the "real" way to play.

Sardinia was much needed, a chance to decompress after everything I'd been through. It wasn't just the beauty of the island or the fun of discovering new cultures—it was the shift in perspective. For the first time in years, I felt like I could breathe, like I wasn't carrying the weight of survival on my shoulders.

As we sailed back to the States, I couldn't help but reflect on how far I'd come—from the jungles of Vietnam to the calm waters of the Mediterranean. Life had a way of throwing curveballs, but through it all, I learned to adapt and find meaning in the chaos. And for now, that was enough.

When we returned to the States, I knew I needed something more than reflection—a way to channel the energy stirring inside me to find purpose again. I didn't know it yet, but that search would eventually lead me to find a new adrenaline fix.

CHAPTER 8

ADRENALINE, HEALING, AND RESILIENCE

The sound of screeching tires filled the air as the car skidded around the final curve. I could feel my heart pounding in my chest and adrenaline surging through my veins. Behind the wheel, I felt alive in a way I hadn't since Vietnam.

Racing wasn't just a sport—it was a lifeline, a way to channel the restlessness that still churned inside me.

But let's back up.

When I left Vietnam, I thought the most challenging part was over. I'd survived the mortar pit, the constant attacks, the sleepless nights. Coming home should've been the easy part. Instead, it was like walking into a world I didn't recognize.

The quiet, the stillness, the way people went about their lives as if nothing had happened—it all felt so foreign to me. I was still fighting battles, but now they were inside me, and no one else could see them.

Transitioning out of the Navy wasn't a clean break. I'd spent my last year on the USS *Fulton*, thrown into a critical role I'd never trained for. At first, the work consumed me—ordering submarine parts and ensuring everything was in place for six-month deployments.

It felt like a continuation of the mission, a way to stay useful. But when my time was up, and I finally stepped off the ship, there was no next mission waiting for me—just silence.

When I left the Navy, I thought I was done with adrenaline. I thought I could pack away the unpredictability and the heart-pounding moments that had defined my time in Vietnam and aboard the USS *Fulton*.

What I didn't realize was that adrenaline wasn't something I could leave behind. It had seeped into my bones, a constant hum beneath the surface of my everyday life. Hockey was out of the question because I was newly married and didn't know anyone in the hockey arena anymore. I was busy making ends meet. Yet it wasn't long before I found myself chasing it again—this time on the racetrack.

***

The call came unexpectedly.

"Larry," Ralph Rue said, his voice a mix of frustration and hope, "I need your help. I can't figure this car out."

Ralph had been struggling ever since the track at Flemington switched from dirt to asphalt. Like so many drivers making the transition, he couldn't find the proper setup. His car was sluggish, tight in the corners, and fighting him every step of the way. For someone as experienced as Ralph, it was humiliating.

I agreed to meet him at the track for a practice session. When I arrived, I gave his car a once-over, walking around it with my hands on my hips. I asked Ralph for his sheets, analyzing every detail of the car down to the bolts that were used.

"Jack it up," I told his crew. "Take off the springs and shocks—and throw them in the garbage."

Ralph's head snapped up. "What? Are you serious?"

"Dead serious," I replied. "You've got this car sprung like it's still running on dirt. This is asphalt. It doesn't work."

Reluctantly, Ralph nodded, and his crew got to work. As they removed the old parts, I explained what we were going to do. "On asphalt, you need a completely different setup. We're changing the springs, the shocks, everything. And trust me, it's going to make all the difference."

Ralph was skeptical, and I couldn't blame him. This wasn't a small adjustment—it was a complete overhaul. But he let me make the changes, and by the time we were finished, his car was ready to hit the track.

This wasn't a small adjustment—it was a complete overhaul.

As he rolled out for practice, I stood on the pit wall, arms crossed, watching intently. The moment Ralph hit the throttle, I could hear the difference. The car wasn't fighting him anymore. It hugged the corners, smooth and fast, the way an asphalt car should.

When he returned to the pits, Ralph climbed out of the car with a huge grin on his face. "Larry," he said, walking over to me, "this car is a rocket ship."

I nodded. "Told you."

That weekend, Ralph lined up for the feature race, his car shining under the track lights. From the drop of the green flag, he dominated. Lap after lap, he pulled farther ahead of the pack. By the time the checkered flag waved, no one else was even close.

As Ralph pulled into Victory Lane, his crew came running down the pit lane, cheering and clapping. One of them stopped in front of me, a huge grin on his face. "Larry, get over here!" he shouted. "Victory Lane! You're part of this, too!"

I hesitated, glancing down at the shirt I was wearing. It was from Jim Romeo's crew; the team I'd been helping that season. Before I could say a word, Ralph's crew tossed me one of their shirts. I pulled it on over my own and jogged toward Victory Lane, where Ralph stood beside his car, waving to the crowd.

The cameras flashed as we posed for pictures, Ralph beaming with pride. Later, he signed one of the photos and handed it to me. "We wouldn't be here without you, Larry," he said. "Thank you."

After that night, Ralph's success only grew. He went on to win four or five more races that season, and every time, he credited the changes we made to the car. His dad would see me at the track and say, "Larry, we'd never be here if it weren't for you."

To me, it wasn't about the credit. It was about the thrill of making a car faster, of watching someone like Ralph finally find his rhythm. Racing has always been about going faster, pushing limits, and figuring out how to get an edge. That's what I did for Ralph, and seeing him succeed was everything.

***

Helping Ralph find his way back to Victory Lane reignited my own determination to get there someday. For years, it felt like an uphill battle. Week after week, season after season, I poured everything I had into my car and the track, but the wins just wouldn't come.

It wasn't for lack of effort—I'd worked my way through different tracks, fine-tuned setups, and taken every lesson I could from veteran racers. But sometimes, no matter how much grit you bring, victory feels just out of reach.

Then, one night, everything changed.

It was a regular Saturday night at White Lake Speedway in upstate New York. The air smelled of burnt rubber and fuel, the stands packed with fans ready for another night of roaring engines. My car, the asphalt-modified beauty I'd been building toward for years, sat in the pit, its engine purring like a caged lion. I'd spent years learning and adjusting, and something about this night felt different—like all the pieces were finally falling into place.

The green flag dropped, and I hit the gas. From the start, the car responded like a dream. Every tweak to the suspension, every adjustment to the tires—it all paid off. Lap after lap, I found my rhythm, weaving through traffic, hitting the corners just right, and holding my line down the straights. The crowd blurred into a roar as I focused on the track ahead.

I wasn't just racing; I was in sync with the car, the track, and myself. It was as if I had finally found my niche.

By the halfway point, I'd taken the lead, and I wasn't giving it up. The car felt unstoppable, sticking to the track like it was glued there. I could feel the tension behind me—other drivers pushing, trying to gain ground—but it didn't matter. Lap after lap, I held my position.

Finally, the white flag waved—one lap to go. My heart pounded as I navigated the final turns, my grip on the wheel tightening with each curve. When I crossed the finish line, the checkered flag waved, and the realization hit me like a tidal wave.

I'd done it.

Thirteen years of racing—thirteen years of setbacks, near-misses, and heartache—all led to this moment. My first feature win.

I pulled into Victory Lane, the crowd on their feet, the announcer's voice booming over the loudspeakers. "You dominated out there to-night! How many wins is this for you?" he asked, shoving a micro-phone toward me.

"This is my first," I replied, grinning so hard my cheeks ached.

The crowd erupted in disbelief. Cheers mixed with gasps, and I could hear people murmuring, "Thirteen years? That's incredible."

That night in Victory Lane, I felt the echoes of all the nights spent in Jim's shop, turning wrenches and learning lessons that weren't just about cars—they were about life. Jim's wisdom had a way of sticking with me, and every adjustment I made on the track that night felt like an extension of what I'd learned in his shop.

It was surreal. Standing there in Victory Lane, holding the trophy, I wasn't just a guy who finally won a race—I was proof that persistence pays off. The years of grinding, tweaking the car, and pushing myself to learn and grow all crystallized into this one moment.

The win wasn't just about crossing the finish line first. It was about everything that led up to it—the failures, the frustrations, the nights spent wrenching on the car until my hands were raw. It was about proving to myself that I could do it, even when the odds seemed stacked against me.

That night, I went to bed with the trophy on the nightstand, my heart full and my spirit renewed. It wasn't just a win; it was a turning point. Every lap I'd ever driven had pointed to this moment.

***

That night felt like the culmination of everything I'd been working toward, but in truth, it was just another step in a much longer journey. Success in racing—and life—doesn't come from a single moment; it's built lap by lap, decision by decision, and often, lesson by hard-earned lesson.

For me, one of the most important lessons came long before that win, in a place that became a second home: Jim's shop. I learned the art of racing in Jim's shop—how every bolt, spring, and shock played a role in creating something greater than the sum of its parts. It wasn't just about fixing cars; it was about understanding them and anticipating problems before they happened. If Victory Lane was the dream, Jim's shop was where the foundation for that dream was built.

Jim's shop was a hive of activity. The walls were lined with tools and parts, and the air was filled with the hum of conversation and the clang of wrenches. For a racer like me, it was Heaven.

I'd first met Jim through the racing community, and we hit it off immediately. He was a seasoned race car owner with a reputation for knowing cars inside and out. His operation wasn't flashy, but it was effective. Jim's cars were consistent winners, and his success wasn't luck—it was the product of meticulous preparation and a deep understanding of how every part of a car worked with every other part.

When I wasn't racing, I spent hours at Jim's shop, soaking up everything I could. He wasn't one to lecture or hold formal lessons. Instead, he'd hand me a wrench, point me toward a car, and let me figure things out under his watchful eye.

"Feel that?" he'd say, handing me a spring. "That's too stiff for this track. Swap it out for a softer one and see how it handles."

At first, I didn't know what the hell I was doing. Sure, I'd grown up around cars, but racing was a different animal. It wasn't just about making a car go fast—it was about making it handle, making it last, making it fit the unique demands of each track and driver. Jim taught me to think about the big picture and see the car as a system where every part had a role.

His approach was holistic. "The car's only as strong as its weakest part," he'd remind me. "If one piece isn't working, the whole system suffers." That perspective changed the way I approached racing—and life.

He also taught me the value of consistency. "Racing's not won on race day," he'd say, tightening a bolt. "It's won in the shop on the nights nobody sees."

We worked on everything together—chassis, suspension, and engines. He showed me how to tune a carburetor for maximum power, adjust the shocks to balance the car, and keep everything running smoothly through the grind of a long season. He didn't just teach me to fix problems—he taught me to anticipate them and think two steps ahead.

It wasn't just technical skills I learned from Jim, though. He had a way of bringing people together. His shop was a gathering place, a home base for racers who wanted to learn, share stories, or just hang out. There was something magnetic about him—his passion, his knowledge, and his easygoing nature. Being around him, you couldn't help but want to be better.

Jim's cars were a benchmark in the local racing scene, and working with him gave me an edge I couldn't have gotten anywhere else. But it also gave me a standard to aspire to. He set the bar high—not just for performance but for preparation, teamwork, and dedication. Everything I accomplished later in my racing career, from helping Ralph to building my own cars, was built on the foundation Jim helped me lay.

While Jim was the foundation, Bruce was a pillar. Bruce's Speed wasn't just a shop—it was a gateway to understanding the business side of racing. He introduced me to the world of vendor shows, sponsorships, and networking, teaching me that racing wasn't just about what happened on the track—it was about what you could build off it.

Years later, when I was standing in Victory Lane or fine-tuning a setup that would give someone their best shot at a win, I'd think back to those nights in Jim and Bruce's shops. Every win—whether it was mine or someone else's—felt like a piece of Jim and Bruce's legacy.

Their lessons weren't just about mechanics or racing. They were about teamwork, preparation, and knowing how to turn setbacks into opportunities. The lessons I learned there didn't just make me a better racer—they made me a better teammate, a better problem-solver, and, in many ways, a better person.

From the track to the shop, every step in my racing journey was another way to push forward, to prove to myself that the lessons I'd learned in Vietnam—about resilience, focus, and camaraderie—weren't limited to the battlefield. They were just as important on the racetrack, and they'd carry me through the rest of my life.

***

The rev of the engines and the rush of adrenaline on the racetrack filled a void I didn't even know I had. Decades after Vietnam, that need for intensity—born in the chaos of war—still pulsed through me as if my body had been rewired to crave the surge of danger and urgency. Racing wasn't just a hobby; it was a way to harness the storm that never fully left me.

Vietnam had been a masterclass in extremes—moments of sheer terror punctuated by seconds of sharp, electrifying focus. That kind of hyper-awareness doesn't just disappear when the war ends. Coming home, I realized my body still needed something to push against, something to channel the energy that had been my survival mechanism. Racing became that outlet. Behind the wheel, every nerve firing, every muscle taut, I found a way to manage the intensity that had once kept me alive.

But racing wasn't just about adrenaline. It was about healing, taking the energy inside me, and giving it purpose. When I was on the track, it wasn't just the car moving forward—I was working through the shadows of my past, one lap at a time. The track taught me something Vietnam hadn't: how to carry intensity without letting it consume me.

But the challenges I faced off the track were often far more daunting. Decades after Vietnam, I was still fighting battles I never signed up for—like the health impacts of Agent Orange. It wasn't just me; so many of us who served came back with invisible wounds, some of which took years to manifest. For me, it was chronic health issues that no doctor seemed to understand, let alone solve. Fifty years of dealing with chronic diarrhea became my new normal, a grim souvenir from the war. It was frustrating, exhausting, and, at times, felt hopeless. But I couldn't let it win.

But adrenaline and Agent Orange were just part of the equation. What people didn't see—what I didn't even fully understand myself for a long time—was the way PTSD shaped everything I did. The war had wired my brain to stay on high alert, to always be ready for the next threat. Even years later, when the only threats were in my head, that wiring stayed. Racing helped. It gave me a sense of control, a focus that quieted the noise.

when I stopped trying to tough it out and actually let people in— things began to change.

But off the track? Relationships, especially, were challenging. I carried an anger I didn't know how to explain, let alone manage. It pushed people away, even the ones who cared about me most.

There were good days and bad days, but over time, I realized I couldn't do it alone. Friends like Carl, who understood what it was like to live with these ghosts, became lifelines. And when I started to open up—when I stopped trying to tough it out and actually let people in—things began to change.

Getting the VA to acknowledge these struggles was its own kind of race. It wasn't just about me—it was about every veteran who felt like they were shouting into the void. The system is complex, slow, and often disheartening, but I learned that persistence was the only way forward. You had to know the right questions to ask, the correct forms to fill in, and, most importantly, you had to keep showing up. Advocating for yourself wasn't just an act of self-preservation—it was a statement that your service, sacrifice, and struggles mattered.

It wasn't like you crossed the finish line and someone handed you a trophy. No, you had to fight for every inch, every benefit, every acknowledgment. But just like on the track, persistence paid off. When I finally started getting the support I needed, it wasn't just a victory for me—it was a reminder that we have to speak up, even when the system feels stacked against us.

The resilience I leaned on in Vietnam followed me to the racetrack and into life after the war. Just like I'd learned to keep going under mortar fire, I pushed through the setbacks and near-misses of racing. Every crash, engine failure, and race I didn't win reminded me that the fight wasn't over. You adapt, you adjust, and you keep showing up.

In racing, as in war, persistence was the difference between standing still and moving forward. It didn't matter how long it took or how many obstacles I hit—I knew I couldn't stop. Thirteen years to Victory Lane might have seemed like a long time to some, but for me, it was just proof that persistence pays off.

Racing also brought people into my life who reminded me of the camaraderie I'd experienced in Vietnam. On the track and in the shop,

I found a sense of connection that mirrored the bonds I'd shared with my fellow soldiers. Jim's shop felt like a home base, much like the makeshift camps we'd built in Vietnam. The track became a community where people like Ralph and Bruce became more than colleagues. They became friends who shared my passion and understood the drive to keep moving forward.

But relationships weren't always easy. PTSD doesn't just create struggles in your mind—it creates struggles in your heart. The anger, the outbursts, the isolation—it all seeped into my marriages and my friendships. Yet, it was relationships that saved me. Friends like Carl, who stayed by my side through thick and thin, and people like Jim and Bruce, who gave me purpose and connection when I needed it most, reminded me that I wasn't alone.

Advocacy became another kind of fight—one in which I learned to speak up not just for myself but also for others. Veterans like Carl, who struggled to get the benefits they deserve, often just needed someone to tell them it was possible. I tried to remind them that they weren't alone, that their service mattered, and that their fight didn't end when they came home.

Carl's still with me today, not just as a friend but as a mirror of the journey we've both taken. We've seen each other at our worst, and somehow, we've always managed to help each other find our way back to solid ground. He's proof that even when life frays your edges, the right relationships can hold you together.

***

Looking back, I think about the idea of "quiet heroes." It's a phrase that resonates deeply with me. In Vietnam, the heroes weren't just the ones pulling the trigger or leading the charge.

They were the guys keeping the radio lines open, the ones patching up wounds under fire and carrying fear but showing up anyway. Quiet heroes aren't flashy—they're relentless. They advocate for themselves, for their brothers, and for what's right, even when the world doesn't seem to care.

That same spirit carried me through racing, through life after the war, and even through the battles I've fought with the VA. Advocating for yourself isn't easy. For veterans like me, it means speaking up when you'd rather stay silent. It means fighting for the benefits you've earned, even when the system makes you feel invisible. It means showing up for yourself, even when it feels like no one else will.

But this isn't just a lesson for veterans—it's for anyone. Whether you're fighting a war, a system, or your own inner demons, being a quiet hero means refusing to give up. It means knowing your worth and standing up for it, even when it feels like the odds are stacked against you.

As I sit here today, I see the connections between the tracks I raced and the jungles I survived more clearly than ever. Vietnam gave me resilience. Racing gave me focus. And the people I've met along the way gave me the strength to keep going, no matter what.

Our battles aren't always loud. Sometimes, they're fought in silence, in the quiet spaces where resilience grows.

Being a quiet hero isn't about medals or recognition—it's about the strength to show up, persevere, and find purpose in uncertainty. Quiet heroes aren't always in the spotlight, but they're the glue that holds everything together. I've carried that lesson with me, both in racing and in life. Being a quiet hero isn't about the recognition—it's about the impact you make, no matter how small it seems in the moment.

It's about the laps you take, the lessons you learn, and the lives you touch along the way. If there's one thing I've learned, it's that we all have the capacity to be quiet heroes—to face the challenges life throws at us, to rise stronger, and to leave the world better than we found it.

But being a quiet hero doesn't mean staying silent or doing it alone. It means showing up for yourself and the people you care about, even when it's hard. It means speaking up, advocating, and refusing to settle for less than you deserve. The battles you've fought—the ones people see and the ones they don't—matter, and your voice matters, too.

Speak up. Share your stories. Whether it's with loved ones, professionals, or even just yourself, letting those experiences out is how healing begins. Advocate for what you need. The support and benefits are there, but don't come to those who stay silent. You must step forward. You must raise your voice.

Quiet heroes aren't born—they're forged in struggle and resilience, in the courage to fight for yourself and others. Being a quiet hero means knowing that even in your quietest moments, your voice carries power. So, use it. Share it. Speak up because your story deserves to be heard.

You've fought battles. You've faced chaos. You've shown up. Now, it's time to fight for what matters most: your voice, your story, and your healing. Speak up because every quiet hero deserves to be heard.

What will you fight for next? Will you raise your voice to remind the world, and yourself, that every quiet hero deserves to be heard?

218

OCF Speedway
2004 Eastern States

CONCLUSION

Today, I'm married to my fourth wife, who shows a true desire to understand my PTSD, how it impacts our life, and how to navigate through the highs and lows of the disorder together. I have spent years in therapy; it's an ongoing process. PTSD is a lifelong disorder that continually needs to be addressed. I no longer take medication for PTSD, nor see a psychologist; however, I do visit a VA counselor and use alternative methods to deal with the PTSD, such as Stellar Ganglion Nerve Blocks.

I now find purpose in traveling in our RV to racetracks around the country, watching hockey on TV, dabbling in antiques, and telling my story to anyone who will listen.

This book is part of that. I've seen too many vets who will not talk about their time in service, not seek help, and who alienate their families since they don't understand what they have been through. One of my psychologists told me to talk about my experiences, and it has helped me immensely. My strongest advice is to seek help—you are NOT in this alone.

THANK YOU FOR READING

Quiet Heroes -Stories from The Frontlines of the Vietnam War

The Extraordinary true story of a young athlete turned war veteran, and his journey through survival, speed, and self-discovery.

CONTINUE THE CONVERSATION

If you believe in the message of this book and would like to share in the ministry of getting this important message out, please consider taking part by:

- Leave a 5-star review on Amazon or other online retailers

- Mention it on your blog, Twitter, Instagram, and Facebook page.

- Suggesting Quiet Heroes to friends and send them to the author's website: www.QuietHeros.com

- Bulk copies can be purchased through the author's website: www.QuietHeros.com or contact the publisher at www.HigherLifePublishing.com

www.ingramcontent.com/pod-product-compliance
Lightning Source LLC
Chambersburg PA
CBHW071425300726
48976CB00004B/1239